PRA

"It's hard to ˙
down, but L·
once again with her novel."

—Erika Sorocco, Teen Correspondent

"A mature, sensitive young adult novel."

—*Eternal Night*

MY ALTERNATE LIFE

"Witty, dramatic, well paced, a page turner. Trinity stands up and lives on the page: gutsy, vulnerable, street-smart, people-smart—okay, just plain smart—a survivor with a heart."

—Nancy Springer, Edgar Award–winning author of *I Am Mordred*

"This is an absolutely refreshing read. McClain writes realistically about fashion, cliques, teenage sexuality and what happens when you're 15 and desperate."

—*RT BOOKclub*

"Lee McClain has created a diamond among cubic zirconia with *My Alternate Life*. Filled with wonderful characters, both main and supporting, as well as an extremely fresh and original plot, this is sure to be a winner in the eyes of teenage readers the world over."

—Erika Sorocco, Teen Correspondent

"*My Alternate Life* was a book that I couldn't put down. Lee McClain has mastered the art of writing a truly heartwarming story that incorporates the humor and irony of life with serious issues."

—*Romance Reviews Today*

THE LANGUAGE OF LOVE

Hector reached for the stack of Spanish *Cosmo*s and pulled one toward me. "Find something you think looks interesting, and we'll talk about it. In Spanish."

"Yeah, right." I thumbed through the magazine, still catching my breath. My thigh seemed to tingle where he'd touched it moments earlier. What would it be like to have those big, gentle hands holding me?

And then I shook my head. It was arrogant Hector Cardona I was fantasizing about. Brianna's boy-friend.

I shoved the magazine at him, opening it blindly to a page. "Here. What's that about?"

Hector studied the page. Red crept up his neck.

"Well, what does it say?"

"It means…'How to dress so he'll want to take it off.'"

Other books by Lee McClain:

MY ABNORMAL LIFE
MY ALTERNATE LIFE

My Loco Life

Lee McClain

SMOOCH NEW YORK CITY

SMOOCH ®

April 2006

Published by

Dorchester Publishing Co., Inc.
200 Madison Avenue
New York, NY 10016

ISBN 0-8439-5661-5

The name "SMOOCH" and its logo are trademarks of Dorchester Publishing Co., Inc.

Printed in the United States of America.

Visit us on the web at www.smoochya.com.

ACKNOWLEDGMENTS

Many thanks to Yolanda Doub, who offered last-minute Spanish translations, and Sandy Garcia-Tunon for her advice on Cuban idioms and family life. All mistakes are, of course, my own. I also appreciate the support and enthusiasm of my mother, Janet Tobin. Thanks, Mom, for being my biggest fan!

My Loco Life

Chapter One

"Alicia Jiminez? New student?" The teacher scanned the classroom over the top of his reading glasses.

"Here," I said.

Beside me, a nasal male voice started humming "Livin' La Vida Loca." The sound was quiet at first, like the buzzing of a fly. But it got louder and louder as the out-of-it teacher continued to call the roll.

Other students turned to see what the noise was all about. The kid beside me must have liked the attention, because he switched from humming to singing. He crooned into a pretend microphone, wiggling his eyebrows at me.

A few of the other students snickered.

I didn't need this, not on my first day at Linden High. Okay, so I have black hair, brown eyes, and a permanent suntan. And I do tend to favor red lip gloss. And my name stands out in western Pennsylvania, which is a long way from the border.

But I'm further than any of these strangers could guess from being a typical Latina.

I stared down at my desk, shaking my hair so it shielded my face.

"Hey, senorita!"

Oh, geez. He was one of those guys who didn't give up. I was gonna have to squash him if I didn't want a rep for weakness.

Another guy, this one in front of me, turned around. He was completely gorgeous: broad shoulders, dark wavy hair, and stubble on his face that told me he already shaved a full beard.

"Es un comemierda, no?" he said, or something like that. A dimple danced in his cheek.

Great. The cutest boy in the entire school speaks to me, and I have no idea what he said. My blush got deeper, and I turned my head away without answering, sneaking another glance at him through my hair.

He looked surprised and almost hurt. Then he shrugged and turned back to face the front.

"Hey, senorita. You deaf?" the jerk beside me said in a stage whisper.

I glanced over at him. "No. I just don't like *little* boys."

A few students laughed. The gorgeous guy in front of me didn't turn around.

"Fiery," said the little guy, smacking his lips.

I stared down at my notebook, tracing over and over a dress design I was working on. I was at one of the only high schools in the state that had a fashion design program. If I did well in it, maybe I could get into a great design school when I graduated.

I'd begged and pleaded for a placement in Linden

Falls, and I was determined to make it work, even though my new foster parents, an engineer and a college professor, intimidated the hell out of me.

The bell rang, finally, and I stood and walked toward the door. The boy who'd been harassing me was waiting. I'd expected that, and I dodged behind another kid and tried to ease out past him.

And collided with the gorgeous Hispanic guy. Since he was so big, he sent me reeling—and caught me with a warm, steadying hand on my shoulder.

"Hey!" I said as my heart rate spiked. "Watch it!"

More rapid-fire Spanish streamed from his lips.

I felt like a complete idiot. Most people assumed I knew Spanish, and you'd think I'd remember at least a little from my birth mother. But no. I couldn't even learn it. I'd tried. Two separate semesters I'd humiliated myself in Spanish One before giving it up as a lost cause.

Okay, I'm no genius. I have to work hard for my Bs. But with most subjects, I get it eventually.

Not Spanish.

All that failure flashed through my mind as the handsome guy's incomprehensible words echoed around me.

"*Entiendes?*" he asked.

I did remember what that meant: *Do you understand?*

The answer was no.

And I didn't want to admit it to this guy. "Why are you talking Spanish to me?" I asked, and then spun away without waiting for an answer.

3

"There goes the spicy senorita!" called the little twerp.

"Is every guy in this school a jerk, or just the ones in this class?" I tossed the words behind me as I flipped back my hair, straightened my shoulders, and marched down the hall.

When I reached the sewing lab, I felt my shoulders loosen. I relished the smell of new fabric, the whirr of sewing machines, the *snip, snip* of scissors, and—how completely great!—a big display of dress sketches in one corner of the room. I felt like I'd come home.

I approached the teacher's desk, handed her my new-kid paperwork, and introduced myself. Here, I wanted to make a good impression.

She smiled distractedly, glanced around the room, and pointed to a table by the windows. "Join table six," she said to me, and then called out, "Katie, please show . . ." She trailed off and glanced at my paperwork again. "Please show Alicia her storage drawer and explain how the class works."

A plump girl with curly brown hair gave me a friendly smile as I approached her table. "Right here," she said, indicating a seat. "Once you get your supplies, you can put them in here." She tapped the cabinet beside the table.

I slid into the chair and put down my books. "Thanks."

"We'll have some time to work on our projects or designs while Mrs. Greene gets organized—" She rolled her eyes. "That can take awhile. And then she'll

4

come around and check on everybody, then we'll have a little lecture, then more time to work."

"Great." I smiled at her. Girls who took sewing weren't usually the hippest chicks at a school, but they were nice. And the structure sounded a lot like Family Science at my last school. Maybe this class would be relaxing.

Katie sat down next to me. "Did you make your vest?" she asked, studying the embroidery.

I nodded.

"Wow, it's really good!"

"If you like that sort of thing," said a voice from across the table.

I looked up into cold blue eyes. A curled lip marred the blonde's prettiness. I could tell her outfit cost more than my entire wardrobe.

"Pleasure to meet you too," I said without bothering to hide my instant dislike.

She snorted.

"Meow, Brianna," said another, male voice, and only then did I notice that the fourth occupant of the table was a thin, stylish boy. His hair stood up in cute blond spikes, and he wielded a pair of pinking shears as if he'd been born using them. "Don't take out your PMS on the new girl."

"You are so gay," she said to him.

He ignored that and turned to me. "That vest *is* primitive," he said. "Kind of sixties. You really made it?"

I couldn't tell if he was teasing me or not, and I felt defensive. I'd worn this vest, along with my slim black

5

skirt, because it was my favorite feel-good outfit. "Yeah, and?"

He lifted his hands, palms out. "Hey, I like the look," he said as he went back to pinning a pattern on some fabric. "I'm Jimmy. Where'd you move from?"

"Pittsburgh."

"Where are you living now?" he asked.

"Grover Street. With the Dashers."

"With the Dashers?" Katie looked puzzled, and then light dawned. "Oh, you're their new foster child!"

"God, we're overrun with them," Brianna said.

My body tensed. They had no idea what it was like to be in foster care. They couldn't have a clue that I was worried sick about my old foster mom, whose health was going downhill fast. And that I was mad at her too, because in the end she'd let the social workers talk her into putting us kids out.

Luckily, the teacher pulled it together and started talking to the whole group, so my table had to shut up. Then everyone got busy with their projects, and since I didn't have any fabric yet, I went over to the design area.

But even there I didn't get any peace. "So you're the new foster kid?" asked an incredibly pretty brunette.

Why did that have to be my defining trait? It had never been an issue in Pittsburgh, where a lot of kids had unusual family situations. But obviously Linden Falls was different. "Yeah, what about it?" I asked.

"No need to be touchy," she said. "I'm Rose. And I'm in the system too. Do you know about Altlives?"

"What?"

"It's a computer game," she said, keeping her voice low like it was some big secret. "It can show you your birth family."

I pulled my head back and stared at her. She didn't look crazy, but talk was telling.

"I know, it sounds wild," she said. "But just in case you're missing someone, it's a way to check in." She must have seen my disbelief, because she laughed a little. "I can show you how to try it. Really. It works."

"Even if it did, I don't have any more interest in my birth family than they had in me," I said.

"Whoa. Fine." She turned away.

I stalked back to my table.

"What'd you say to Rose?" Jimmy asked when I arrived. "She looks pissed."

"She's nuts, right?"

"Not the last I heard," he said. "Look, here comes Brianna, and let me advise you, do not piss her off. She has the sharpest claws in the school."

The teacher was with Brianna, and as they headed our way, they were talking intently about something. Scheming, from the looks of things. "Make sure your sample garment is on the conservative side," the teacher was saying. "They like to see that you can do classic design."

"Gearing up for that scholarship, Brianna?" Jimmy asked. "Look out—I might go for it myself. I'd love to go to Europe."

"In your dreams." She bent over her drawer and rummaged through it. "I had my sketch in here somewhere. . . . Now where is it?"

"What scholarship?" I asked.

"It's early admission to this design school in Madrid," Jimmy explained.

"The International Institute of Fashion Design," Katie threw in. "You know, IIFD."

I gasped. That was one of the best design schools in the world.

"A full ride," Jimmy continued. "But don't even try, because we all know Brianna's going to get it."

"Now, Jimmy. Anyone can compete." The teacher frowned fondly at both him and Brianna.

"Did you say early admission? Like, before high school is over?" My heart started beating really fast. If I could be settled somewhere like that before I aged out of foster care, I'd be a million times closer to my dream.

The teacher nodded.

"What do I have to do to apply?"

She raised an eyebrow. "Design and produce an exceptional garment, first of all," she said. "And write an essay about your career goals. There's an application, and some other requirements, but the main thing is the garment, obviously."

"It's really competitive," Katie said.

"And classic, not primitive." Brianna shot a sneer in the direction of my outfit.

"Linden High has had a student accepted every year for the past ten years," Mrs. Greene said. She patted Brianna's shoulder.

"Where can I get an application?"

"Oh! Well, I suppose I can get you one if you're interested. . . ." She hesitated, tried and failed to remember my name, and settled for "dear" and a vague smile.

As she walked away, Brianna studied me with open hostility. "Don't think you'll get it just because you're all Spanish and everything."

I started to correct her. Spanish, as in from Spain, was one nationality I was pretty sure I wasn't. But I didn't want to get into my mysterious background with this nosy crowd. "What's Spanish got to do with winning?" I asked instead.

"God, if you don't know—" Brianna started.

"Were you planning to make it on your people skills?" I interrupted, treating her to a fake smile.

Katie giggled.

"What are *you* laughing at?" Brianna snarled, adding an ugly and totally inappropriate name that made Katie gasp.

In a flash I was around the table, cupping Brianna's chin in my hand. "Listen," I said right in her face, "this is my table now too, and you don't insult my friends."

"Let go of me!" Her shrill voice echoed in the suddenly quiet room. She swiped long fingernails down my arm.

I yanked it back and stared at the red welts rising on my skin. Then I started to shove her, but Jimmy grabbed me from behind.

"Girls!" Mrs. Greene hurried over. "What's this all about?"

Neither of us said anything. We were too busy staring each other down.

"Just a little artistic rivalry," Jimmy said. "It's healthy, Mrs. Greene."

"And it can get you ousted from class," she said. "This is an elective, and being here is a privilege. You ladies had better not forget it."

"May I go to the bathroom?" Brianna asked, her eyes wide and blue and full of crocodile tears.

"Of course." Mrs. Greene patted her shoulder.

I had to admire Brianna's tactics. She knew how to get Mrs. Greene's sympathy. As the new girl, I would be suspected of starting the fight, of course.

"I'm sorry," I said after Brianna left. "I won't cause any more trouble."

"See that you don't." Mrs. Greene's lips tightened into a narrow line, and this time she didn't call me "dear." She turned and walked away.

Katie gave me an anxious smile. "Thanks for standing up for me, but it's best to just ignore Brianna," she said.

"And see, I wasn't kidding about claws," Jimmy added, looking at my arm. "You'd better get some antibiotic on those scratches, girlfriend."

"What did she mean about me being Spanish?"

"Knowing Spanish would help you get the scholarship, since IIFD is in Madrid," Katie explained.

"Oh. Right." Gloom swept over me.

"No wonder Brianna's sweating," Jimmy said. "She's been taking it all through school, but she can't compete with a native speaker."

Which wouldn't be me.

I wanted the scholarship so badly that my heart was

pounding. A chance to start design school early. To get out of this infantile high school life and pursue my dreams.

What a cruel joke that it required me to learn Spanish. Completely impossible, from all my previous experience.

But impossible or not, I'd just have to do it.

Chapter Two

"Ah!-ah-ah-ah-ah. Livin' la vida loca!"

I couldn't believe that stupid old song was still haunting me the next Saturday afternoon as I tried to concentrate on my Spanish homework. After finding out about the scholarship, I'd screwed up my courage and signed up for beginning Spanish.

When I finally convinced the teacher that I wasn't just shooting for an easy A, that I actually didn't know Spanish and wanted to learn, I'd gotten into the class.

One week later, I was lost.

The simple nouns and elementary dialogue swam around in front of my eyes, and the blaring music from next door wasn't helping. So I was glad when my foster parents, Betsy and Ray, knocked on my door.

"Ready for a fiesta?" Ray asked, dancing around as Ricky Martin continued to sing.

"Not exactly," I said. "This nineties music is driving me crazy."

Betsy shook her head, smiling, as Ray continued to jump and spin. "He's the crazy one," she said in a stage whisper.

Ray spun his finger around his ear and kept on dancing.

Ray was different from any man I'd ever encountered. You could tell he was brilliant from listening to his offhand explanations of things he read or projects he was working on. He was an engineer and must have had an important job, because he seemed to bring home lots of money.

But off the job he was always hamming it up and joking around.

Betsy, my new foster mom, had big blue eyes and a concerned expression most of the time. She was a part-time English professor at a nearby college.

We were all on good behavior around each other. I was trying to appreciate them even though I missed my old foster mom and my city neighborhood. And they were trying to get used to a different kind of teenager from their own two superstar scholars.

Even though their high expectations worried me, I knew I was lucky. I'd had one placement from ages three to fifteen, with a loving foster mom and just a couple of other kids. Now my second placement was good too. I'd heard enough foster-kid horror stories to know I'd been blessed.

"Come on," Betsy said. "We're going to the party next door!"

"The Vida Locas?"

Ray grinned and nodded. "We've been neighbors with the Cardona family since we moved here, oh what, twelve years ago?" He looked at Betsy.

"That's right, and they're very excited to meet you."

"The feeling isn't mutual," I muttered under my breath. I walked over to the window. Through the green-budded tree branches, I could see the backyard next door. It was full of people grilling and talking and having a great time.

And I didn't know a one of them. "Do we have to go?" I blurted out.

"Aw, honey, it'll be fun," Betsy said, coming over to put an arm around me. "There's at least one boy about your age. And they're all just the nicest people."

"Good food too," Ray said.

I saw a gang of adorable kids running around. Maybe I could score babysitting jobs and make some cash for clothes. "Okay," I said. "I'll go."

But I regretted agreeing as soon as we opened the Cardonas' gate. "Are they speaking Spanish?" I asked.

Betsy smiled. "Yes, isn't that wonderful! The Cardonas are from Cuba. That's one reason why we felt we were a good match for you. There's an opportunity to share your culture right here in the neighborhood!"

My culture, baloney. My culture was inner-city Pittsburgh, not the colorful, stylish bilingual world that blared from this backyard.

But we were here, and the friendly Cardonas were

15

already descending on us. To me, their smiles looked like bared teeth, their numbers as big as an enemy army.

Fortunately they switched to English to greet me and congratulate Betsy and Ray on being so kind as to take in a pretty girl like me. "And she doesn't have a family!" I heard someone say in a pseudowhisper. *"Que lastima!"*

Ugh. I hated pity, so when a three-year-old with frosting-covered hands ran smack into me, I was glad for the distraction.

"Isabella, no, no!" clucked a gray-haired woman. She looked around and handed me a napkin. *"Lo siento,"* she said to me.

"It's okay." I didn't even bother to scrub the white streak off my black capris. Instead I squatted down to see the little girl eye to eye. "You're Isabella?" I asked her.

She nodded, licking her fingers. "Who you?"

"I'm Alice. Alicia," I corrected myself immediately. I'd been Alice in my first foster family, but the name on my birth certificate and all my paperwork was Alicia. And since I'd moved here, Betsy and Ray had been calling me Alicia with the Spanish pronunciation: Ah-LEE-see-ah.

"I got a Barbie piano," Isabella said. "Want to see?"

Did I ever. "Sure," I said, taking her hand and following her with a shrug and a smile to the assembled adults.

I couldn't believe I had the bad luck to live next door to a big Cuban family. I knew they'd find it appalling I didn't know my culture. And I knew I could never fit in with a group like this, even though they seemed to be having an awful lot of fun.

For just a minute, I let myself indulge in self-pity. Would I ever find a place where I belonged?

Luckily, little Isabella quickly distracted me from those kinds of thoughts. She had a princess-themed bedroom full of toys, and she was obviously used to being the center of attention. She directed me to sit down and be quiet, and continued bossing me around for a good half hour before I heard voices coming down the hall.

"Mami!" Isabella said.

The door was flung open and a barrage of Spanish greeted us. My stomach twisted with anxiety.

And then I looked up and almost choked, because there was the kid from my class. The gorgeous one. The Spanish speaker.

Oh, no. Did he really live next door?

He didn't smile when he saw me. "Hi," he said with no inflection.

"Hi," I said.

"Hector!" Isabella tried to pull him down to play with us, but he resisted with a sharp line of Spanish that made her narrow shoulders slump.

The two women who seemed to have dragged him there went off into another scolding volley of words. He muttered a few things back, but mostly let them talk.

Then they asked me a question. In Spanish, of course.

I pretended I didn't hear, bending my head toward Isabella, but she nudged me and pointed to her mother and said something in Spanish herself.

Even the three-year-old was bilingual. Didn't that just figure?

The woman in red nudged Handsome Hector and repeated the question, looking at me, eyebrows raised.

"She doesn't like Spanish, Tía Julia," he said.

Both women frowned. Isabella's mother looked ready to grab her away from me.

"That's not true," I protested. "Um, *no entiendo Español*." I blushed, knowing my accent was atrociously bad.

That set off another rapid volley of Spanish between the two women, along with a lot of head-shaking and clucking and patting me on the shoulder. In the midst of it, Hector tried to slip off down the hall, but his aunt Julia reached out an arm and grabbed him back.

Isabella's mom, who must also be Hector's mom, took my hand and pointed to herself. *"Me llamo Maria,"* she said slowly, like you'd speak to a little kid. *"Como te llamas?"*

I was pretty sure they were asking me my name. "Alice," I said. "Alicia."

"No, no. Dices, Me llamo Alicia," she said.

My cheeks went hot and my stomach churned. She was trying to teach me Spanish right here and now, in front of a bilingual three-year-old and gorgeous Hector, who already scorned me. Something about these dark-haired people and all this Spanish noise just plain freaked me out.

"I have to go," I said, and pushed my way past them and down the hall, hearing their voices rise in incomprehensible chatter behind me.

I made it to our backyard, then realized I was locked out of the house. But no way was I going back there to get my foster parents. I sank down on the steps, glad for the time alone to figure out my hurt feelings.

But my solitude didn't last. The backyard gate opened, and I was surprised to see Hector letting himself in. "You okay?" he asked as he approached me.

So he was nicer than I'd thought. "I'm fine," I said. "Why?"

He shrugged. "They wanted me to check on you."

My improving attitude took a nosedive. "Okay, you checked. I'm fine."

He ignored me, propped one foot up on a concrete porch step, and stared off into the trees that lined the house.

Great. He was over here out of obligation, and now he was acting like I wasn't even around. "Um, I was hoping for some privacy?" I said.

"Look, just bear with me for another minute. I'll get in trouble if I go back right away. In fact, they want me to bring you back."

"Why?"

"Because," he said, "you don't have a family and we're supposed to be nice to you."

I rolled my eyes. "I don't need your pity."

"And," he said, sounding disgusted, "you're a nice Latina girl who wears modest clothes and likes kids. So they're shoving me at you as an alternative to . . ." He trailed off.

"To what?" My mind raced. His family was pushing him toward me? Me, the family-less, ignorant foster kid?

His handsome mouth twisted. "As an alternative to my girlfriend. Who I'm not allowed to see anymore, just because I made one little mistake."

"What was it?"

He shook his head. "You don't want to know." He slouched down onto the steps beside me. "I actually don't know how I'm going to tell Brianna we can't go out anymore. She's going to kill me. She's very touchy."

The breath whooshed out of me. "Did you say Brianna? Blond Brianna?"

He nodded. "Brianna Davis. You know her?"

"I . . . I've met her."

Thinking about Brianna brought back all the events of last week's sewing class. I'd learned what I could about the early-admission scholarship to IIFD, and it sounded like everything I could want. It would be perfect; it would make my career. But more than half of the classes were conducted in Spanish, so proficiency in the language was a condition of getting in.

After the week I'd had in Spanish One, I'd about given up. But suddenly, a plan came together. "I know how to get your parents off your case if you'll do something for me," I said.

"How? What?" His voice was skeptical, but his brown eyes held a tiny hope.

"I'll pretend to be your girlfriend," I said, "if you'll teach me Spanish."

His eyebrows shot up. "You hot for me?"

"Would you just listen a minute?" I glared at him. "I'm *not* hot for you."

"If you're not trying to jump my bones, what's the point?" he said with a cocky grin and a sparkle in his eyes.

"Are you always so full of yourself?"

"Comes with the good looks."

"Listen," I said, ignoring his dimple, "it's a way to distract them. Make them think you're busy with me all the time. You can take me out, spend an hour tutoring me, and then go see Brianna."

"If you haven't learned Spanish by now, why do you want to?"

I was about to tell him about the design school scholarship. Just in time, I stopped myself.

If he was Brianna's boyfriend, he'd undoubtedly heard about it from her, and he couldn't be so disloyal as to help someone else win her prize.

I felt a mean little thrill about double-crossing that witch with her own boyfriend.

But I couldn't tell Hector that. "I just feel like part of

21

myself is missing, not speaking the language of my roots," I said, making my eyes wide and sad. "Like today. With your family. I felt so out of it." That, at least, was no lie.

"Well . . ." He was a little hooked, I could tell, but unsure.

I studied him, thinking fast. He didn't want his family to push him at me; he wanted to be in control.

"If you don't want to work with me, it's okay," I said, smiling innocently at him. "Maybe someone else in your family could tutor me. I'd like to get to know them better."

"Don't get involved with them," he said instantly. "They'll take over your life."

"But if you don't want to help . . ."

"No, no, I'm thinking about it. It's just . . . Brianna couldn't find out. She's really jealous."

That suited my plans perfectly. "I have no problem keeping it quiet," I said.

He looked at me hard, like he was trying to decide what my game was. I kept my eyes on his.

Birds trilled around us, and the hyacinths beside the back steps sent up a sweet scent. A cool breeze swept by, ruffling my hair.

That must have been what caused the little quiver up and down my spine.

"Okay, then," he said finally, cocking his head to one side as if he wasn't too sure what he'd just agreed to do. His eyes rested on me with a kind of surprised curiosity in them, like he was really seeing me for the first time.

I felt like shouting it for all the world to hear! With Hector's help, maybe I could learn Spanish.

If the egotistical hunk didn't drive me crazy first.

Chapter Three

"Let's get this over with," I told my aging-hippie of a
social worker, Fred.

He'd insisted on meeting me on school property instead of at home for our first post-placement visit. He
probably wanted me to feel free to tell him if Betsy
and Roy were beating up on me. Which of course
they weren't.

Fred gave me the creeps because he'd taken me
away from my first foster mom, and because he had
these weird, all-knowing eyes.

I didn't really like advertising my status as a foster
child at school, especially since it seemed to be such
big news in Linden Falls. So I'd chosen the library for
our visit, thinking no one else would be there after
classes.

Was I ever wrong.

The first person I saw was my Spanish teacher, Mrs.
Leaf. She waved at me and started setting up chairs in
a circle.

Then I realized that a few more students were at

the computers. So Fred and I wouldn't have this place to ourselves.

At least Fred had chosen an out-of-the-way table, over by the windows and half-blocked by shelves of books. But as I approached him, I realized he wasn't alone.

Rose, the girl from my design class who'd tried to tell me about the computer game that allegedly showed people their birth families, was chatting with Fred in a friendly way.

When I approached, her friendliness evaporated. "She won't be interested," she said to Fred, looking at me like I was some kind of criminal.

"What's your problem?" I asked her.

"I don't have a problem," she said. "If you don't care about your family, you're the one with the problem."

"Rose." Fred gave her a meaningful look. "Everyone has a different background. And her own path."

"Sure." She shrugged and said, "Later," without looking at me again.

"Let's get this over with," I said to Fred. "What do you know about my mom?"

"You mean Mrs. Simpson? Or Betsy?"

"Mrs. Simpson. My foster mom."

Fred tapped his pencil on the closed manila folder in front of him. "She's having more tests."

"For what?" My heart started thumping in a heavy rhythm. "Is she sicker?"

"We're not sure. I'll let you know when we get some definitive answers."

He seemed evasive, and I didn't know if I wanted to

know why. On the one hand, I suspected that she wasn't really sick at all, just sick and tired of us kids. The three of us were teenagers, and sometimes we'd been a handful.

On the other hand, she had emphysema and had been smoking all her life, and she was old.

I shied away from where my brain was taking me. "Are Champ and Lia doing okay?"

My longtime foster brother, Champ, had been in too much trouble to get a placement, and had landed in a group home. My foster sister, who'd only been with us for a year, had bounced to a family on the North Side.

"They're fine. Lia got on the cheerleading squad."

"Already?" I smiled, pleased for her. She was great at that stuff.

He nodded. "Last-minute vacancy. And we're still working on a home for Champ."

"Can I visit everybody?"

"After things settle down." He put a hand over mine—I was tearing a piece of paper to shreds. "Alicia. I'm here to talk about *your* placement."

"Yeah, what about it?" My heart pounded again. "Do they hate me or something?"

"No," he said, and flipped open the folder in front of him. "Betsy and Ray think everything's fine. What do you think?"

I sighed, relieved. "It's great. They're nice."

"Can I have some details?" He smiled.

So I told him about Betsy's good cooking and how Ray talked to me about his work and what he read in the paper. I didn't add that Betsy's brown rice and vegetables tended to upset my stomach, or that I couldn't understand half of what Ray said. I wanted to stay, and that meant putting a good face on things.

"Ah, yes. Ray's into string theory. Alternate universes. Extra dimensions." Fred's eyes got even dreamier than usual.

"I know. He's really smart. Does that mean they'll put me out if I flunk a class?"

"No. But what are you flunking?"

I sighed. "Spanish. Again." We'd had a quiz today, and I'd bombed it. My mind had gone completely blank. "I just can't get languages. My brain doesn't work like that."

"Whoa." Fred looked alarmed and held up his hands. "Don't tell your brain that, it'll believe you. You need to speak positively about your abilities. Even if you're just talking to yourself."

I rolled my eyes.

"Why don't you join the Spanish Club?" he suggested.

I waved my hands at him. "Did you not hear me? I'm flunking Spanish. And I hate it. Why would I put myself through that torture in my spare time?"

He shrugged. "If your teacher knows you're trying, it could help. Besides, maybe you're pushing too hard. If you could be involved with Spanish in a fun way, it might go more easily."

"I don't even know if this school *has* a Spanish club."

"They're meeting right over there," he said, gesturing toward the other side of the library.

I looked. Sure enough, a bunch of students had joined Mrs. Leaf.

Including Hector, who was looking right at me.

He was in the Spanish club?

My skin started tingling in the most annoying way. Hector's stare held my eyes and wouldn't let them go. A slow smile came to his lips.

What would it be like to kiss him?

His smile got wider, as if I'd mentally telegraphed my question his way.

Ooh, what was I thinking? He was totally arrogant. I had no desire to kiss him. In fact, I had no desire to interact with him at all, which was why I hadn't followed up on our tutoring arrangement, even though my need was becoming more obvious every day.

"You might want to think about why you push so hard away from your native language," Fred said.

I broke my gaze away from Hector, blushing. "What?"

"It's very likely you heard and spoke Spanish for the first three years of your life," Fred said. "I wonder why it's so hard for you to pick it up now."

"I have no idea," I said.

"There's a way you could learn about your past." Fred turned to the library computer right next to him and started typing something in.

A moment later, there was a video on-screen: a bunch of dark-haired people working in a field. The quality was low, with lots of white spots all over the monitor. He fiddled around with the sound and then the screen went dark, but I could hear some rapid Spanish.

The sound made me want to cover my ears. But I forced myself not to react. I didn't want to give old Fred any more material for his "Sixty Ways Alicia's Screwed Up" file.

He switched back to the bad video and smiled his weird elvish smile.

"What is it?" I asked, trying for politeness. "A news show?"

"This," he said, "is a window into your birth family's world."

"What, like a documentary?"

Slowly, he shook his head. "No. It's an actual window."

Great. My social worker was looney tunes. "Hello? I don't even know what country I was born in!"

He studied the screen again. "Looks like the desert southwest to me," he said. "See the saguaros?" He pointed to a couple of big cactuses in the background.

"Yeah, and?"

"I'm guessing you come from Mexico," he said.

"So you're telling me that this is my birth family? On this computer screen?"

He smiled. "Exactly."

I'd been trying to stay patient, aware that I needed to keep a good relationship with Fred. I wanted to keep this placement, so I needed him to say positive things about me to whatever judge was in charge of my case. But this was too much. The guy was insane!

He must have read my skepticism. " 'There are more things in heaven and earth,' " he said, " 'than are dreamt of in your philosophy.' That's a quote from *Hamlet*, but just ask your foster dad. He knows the universe isn't exactly what it seems to be."

I looked away, trying to regain my patience with this nut. Across the library, the Spanish Club was breaking into smaller groups. Hector stood up, and Brianna was at his side. As I watched, she wrapped her arms around him.

I looked away and my eyes focused on the computer screen. A stooped middle-aged woman tried to lift a heavy bag, then gave up, her hands going to her lower back.

A man with salt-and-pepper hair and bad teeth came over, smiling, and swung the sack to his shoulder. They walked off the field together, silhouetted in the setting sun.

I stood up, marched over to the computer, and hit the power button, ignoring the sign next to it that read, PLEASE DO NOT SHUT DOWN COMPUTERS.

"I have to go," I gritted out to Fred, and then stomped out of the library.

Chapter Four

"Over here, Alicia!"

Nerves assailed me as I walked across Tommy's Pizzeria that night. On the one hand, I was glad Katie and Jimmy had invited me out. I needed friends, as my foster parents kept reminding me.

On the other hand, I hadn't realized this was where everyone from Linden High hung out. The noise was high, and as I slid into a booth beside Katie, I heard someone humming "La Cucaracha" and realized that even the twerp from my American Government class was there.

To torment me.

"Hey," I said to them. "Thanks for asking me."

"Sure." Katie nodded toward the twerp, who was now singing in our direction and strumming an air guitar. Undoubtedly a mariachi one. "What's up with him?" she asked.

"He likes to drive me crazy," I said, ignoring the giggles of his twerpy friends.

"Maybe he likes you."

"Come on," Jimmy said. "Ralphie Mixon is as gay as I am."

"He is *not!*" Katie looked offended. "He's asked me out before."

"Cover," Jimmy explained.

As they argued about it, I breathed in the smell of greasy pizza and shifted to avoid a ripped spot in the booth's faux-leather bench. Between the dinging of video games, Gwen Stefani on the jukebox, and the din of at least forty kids, I could barely hear my new friends anyway.

Friends. I hoped that was why they'd invited me.

When the waitress came, I asked for a Coke and agreed to go in on the veggie pizza they'd already ordered.

After she left, they both turned to focus on me. "So, how serious are you about the IIFD scholarship?" Jimmy asked.

Before I could answer, Katie chimed in. "Brianna's got the idea that you're serious competition," she said. "Are you?"

My guard went up. "Why do you want to know?"

"She's totally wigging out," Katie said.

Jimmy gestured with his Sierra Mist. "We're kind of caught in the crossfire. And with Brianna, that's a scary place to be."

"Look, just stay out of it," I said, scooting a little bit away from them. "Tell her you don't know anything."

"But we *want* to know," Katie said.

"Come on, spill," Jimmy added.

"No way!" I fished under the table for my purse.

34

"My business is my own business. You didn't have to invite me here to find that out."

"Oh, Alicia," Katie said, her voice as warm as her hand on my arm. "Don't go. We want to be your friends!"

"Yeah, we really like you," Jimmy said sarcastically. Katie smacked him.

"What? We do!"

"She doesn't know your sense of humor yet." Katie turned back to me. "Listen, it's just that Brianna has this terrible home life. I probably shouldn't talk about it, but it's pretty obvious to most people."

"Katie's mom's the guidance counselor," Jimmy explained as the waitress brought our pizza.

Katie grabbed a big piece, lifting it high to break the strands of melting cheese. "Mmm, this smells fantastic."

"Now, how many points is it?" Jimmy asked her as he helped himself.

"It's like six, meanie." She slapped at him, then explained, "I'm trying to do Weight Watchers online."

"And I'm trying to keep her honest. But go ahead, Alicia, have some. I'm guessing you're not on a diet."

I took a piece. "So anyway, Brianna has a bad home life so you feel sorry for her?" I asked. "You're on her side?"

"I just know she's motivated," Katie said.

"As in *really* motivated." Jimmy wiped his mouth. "She'd do anything, and I do mean anything, to get that scholarship. So watch your back."

"Well, I'm motivated too," I said.

But their words made me nervous. I could deal with conflict, but that didn't mean I liked it. I already knew that Brianna was a major rival, just from how bitchy she acted toward me. Now I wondered how far she would go to win. Would she sabotage my stuff? Spread bad rumors about me?

Physically hurt me?

Suddenly, the sound of "Livin' La Vida Loca" came rattling over the jukebox. I couldn't help glancing over at the twerp, and then I wished I hadn't. He and his friends were all watching me, and when I looked their way, they all started laughing.

"God, what is the deal with Ralphie?" Jimmy asked. "I never knew he had this thing about Ricky Martin."

"It's not about Ricky Martin, it's about Alicia," Katie said.

Jimmy shook his head. "You *would* think that. You're so naïve."

Katie's eyes narrowed. "Tell you what," she said. "I'll bet you a . . . something . . . I can get him to go out with me before you can get him to go out with you." She turned to me. "Unless you want him," she added anxiously.

"No, thanks," I said.

"You're on," Jimmy said. "Though I think I should get double the whatever if I win. Because I'd be bringing him out of the closet as well as just getting a date."

"Deal," she said. "How about a gift certificate for Smithmore's?"

"No way," Jimmy said. "I wouldn't be caught dead in their fake Kenneth Cole shirts."

"Sssh! Look!" Katie nodded toward the door and then looked away, grabbing another slice of pizza.

I looked, and my heart jumped up and down a couple of times before settling down to a steady thud.

Hector.

With Brianna.

Everyone watched them walk across the restaurant, even though people pretended not to. There was a quiet at first, then a lot of whispering.

I told myself I was just feeling curious. "Why's everyone looking at them?"

"Well, for one thing, that Hector is a gorgeous hunk of manhood," Jimmy said.

"And he's definitely on *our* team, if you know what I mean," Katie said, smirking.

"You're right. And it's a tragedy."

"Thing is, I know he and Brianna broke up," Katie said. "So why's she hanging on him?"

I didn't let them in on the fact that Hector's family was making him break up with her. I knew he'd rather keep that little nugget to himself. Besides which, he was obviously ignoring their instructions.

"He's gorgeous, but not very bright," Jimmy said. "Brianna's bad news."

"Hector is one of those guys who likes to rescue vulnerable women," Katie said, her eyes dreamy.

"Brianna's about as vulnerable as a saber-toothed tiger," I muttered, causing Jimmy to snort out some Sierra Mist.

"Did I hear you say my name?"

I looked up to see Brianna standing beside our table, arms crossed. My eyes flicked around looking for Hector. I spotted him across the room, talking to a table full of guys.

I couldn't help it; Brianna intimidated me. She was so cold and confident, and so able to cut people down with one stroke from her waspish tongue. I couldn't think of how to answer her.

"Everyone's talking about you and Hector," Jimmy said, and I shot him a grateful glance for saving me.

"Oh, yeah?"

"Didn't you guys break up?" Katie asked.

"No, though someone started that rumor." She gave me a baleful look, as if it had been me. "We're together, and we're staying together. No matter who moved in next door to him."

Both Jimmy and Katie turned to me. "You're next door to Hector?"

I nodded.

"But he's mine," Brianna said, "no matter what some wretched Mexican foster girl wants."

I surged to my feet, but two large, warm hands pressed me back down.

"It's not right to blame anyone for her family situation," rumbled Hector's deep voice behind me. "You should know that, Bri."

To my surprise, Brianna blushed red. I was feeling a little warm myself from his touch.

"Come on," Hector said. "Marcus and Jodi saved

seats for us." And the two of them disappeared across the room.

Leaving me to fan myself and calm down.

"Aw, that was so sweet of him," Katie said. "See, he *does* have a thing for vulnerable women."

"Yeah, but Alicia's gonna pay for that little save," Jimmy said. "Brianna's pissed."

"Well, she shouldn't be. That was a really mean thing for her to say." Katie reached over to touch my arm. "And I, for one, am ready to help you get that scholarship. Just tell me what you need."

"Thanks."

"Yeah, Brianna's bitchy," Jimmy agreed. "But just think. If Alicia gets the scholarship and Brianna doesn't, we'll be stuck with Bri for the rest of our high school years. Maybe we should help *her* get it."

"Thanks a lot," I said, hurt.

Katie hit him. "Stop kidding around," she told him. "Tell her you'll help."

"I'll help," Jimmy said, grinning at me. "What do you need? What's your strategy?"

"To pass Spanish, first of all," I said glumly.

"You don't know it already?" Katie looked surprised. "I mean, with your name and your looks and everything, I thought . . ."

I shook my head. "I've spent most of my life in Pennsylvania, raised by families who didn't speak Spanish." I didn't go into the fact that I'd supposedly heard Spanish up until I was three. To me it seemed shameful that my birth family had given me up at that age. They'd had time to get to know me, and had still put me out.

"I don't know if we can help with that," Katie said. "Jimmy and I are both taking French."

"I've got a plan," I said, glancing over toward Hector. "I think."

"What is it?" Jimmy followed my gaze. "Oh, man. This is rich. You want to learn from Hector."

"Well, he is a native speaker," Katie said, her voice conveying a tactful skepticism. "But would he be willing to do that?"

"Would he be allowed?" Jimmy asked. "Bri keeps his choke chain pretty tight."

Their attitude galled me. Maybe it was partly because I wasn't sure myself. He'd agreed, but we hadn't made any plans for tutoring and I was drowning fast in Spanish. "I can get him to help me."

"Go ask him," Jimmy said.

"She can't ask him now, in front of everybody."

"If you go ask him," Jimmy said, "I'll go ask Ralphie out." He smirked at Katie. "And I'll win our bet."

I couldn't get a handle on Jimmy, whether he was my friend or my enemy. But I was tempted to take him up on his dare.

"Bri did just go to the bathroom," Katie said. "And Hector's going over to play Pod."

I glanced over, confirmed what she'd said, and then raised my eyebrows at Jimmy. "I wouldn't mind a gift certificate to Smithmore's, or wherever," I said. "I need some new clothes."

He grinned, looking delighted. "You're on. Who-

MY LOCO LIFE

ever gets a date first gets gift certificates from the other two. Twenty dollars each."

"Hey, wait a minute," Katie complained. "I don't even have a chance."

"Ralphie's fair game for you too," Jimmy said, standing up. "But I'm faster."

"Hey, no fair!" Katie scooted back in her chair and stuffed the rest of her pizza into her mouth.

I stood too. I'd been procrastinating about making an arrangement with Hector, mainly out of being shy. With Jimmy and Katie egging me on, maybe I could do it.

I walked over toward the video games. Hector leaned toward one of them, arms propped in a way that showed his muscles bulging from his T-shirt. Man, he was good-looking! My heart pounded hard.

Hector turned to look at me. At the same moment, I heard Ralphie's nasal voice behind me. "Aw, ain't that cute. The two Mexes getting together. Hey, I saw you eyein' him in study hall. You hot for him?"

I was pretty sure practically the whole restaurant heard.

Including Hector.

And Brianna, who emerged from the bathroom, hairbrush still in hand.

I froze. My heart seemed to stop.

And it seemed like there was this strange little moment of silence in the pizzeria too. Even the jukebox chose that moment to end a song.

Into the silence came Jimmy's voice. "Talk about hot, Ralph baby," he said with an exaggerated lisp. "You have got some prize thighs in those jeans."

41

Laughter and jeers erupted around the restaurant.

Katie headed for Brianna. "Is that lipstick in your teeth?" she asked in a concerned-but-completely-audible whisper. It was the one remark guaranteed to make an appearance-conscious girl like Brianna turn back toward the restroom immediately.

My new friends' words and actions got me back into motion. Acting like nothing strange was happening, I strolled over to the video game next to Hector and reached into my pocket for money. Blindly I fed it into the game, never glancing at the hunk beside me.

I couldn't block out his words, though. "You a big fan of Babes in Toyland?" he asked. I looked up to see the near-naked girls decorating the game.

"For all you know, yes." I started pushing buttons, ignoring the way his eyes seemed to bore into my side. And I kept ignoring him until Brianna came up and reined him back to her side.

Chapter Five

"Alicia, *querida,* can you come help me get lunch on the table? It's tamale casserole."

I waved to Mrs. Cardona, who was visible through the kitchen window, and then I called Isabella out of her playhouse. It was Saturday, and I was entertaining Isabella so that Mrs. Cardona could get ready for a big family dinner the next day.

For just a moment, a fantasy overtook me. What if Mrs. Cardona were *my* mother, my birth mother? What if Isabella were my little sister? What if I belonged smack in the middle of this big, noisy, loving family?

Then I shook myself out of it. My family couldn't have been more different from this one. Isabella was completely adored, a little princess, spoiled and petted by everyone.

When I was Isabella's age, my family had given me away.

"Come on!" My voice came out sharper than I expected.

43

Isabella's face looked serious as she came out of her playhouse. "Whatsa matter, Alicia? You look mad."

"I'm not mad, but it's time for lunch. You should come when I call you."

I shepherded her toward the back stoop, at which point she saw her tiny rake and shovel and headed for the small flower garden beneath the kitchen window. "Come dig with me," she said, giving me a dimpled smile.

"No." I went to the kitchen door and held it. "We can play more after lunch. *If* you do what I say now."

Isabella's lower lip stuck out, but she flounced inside. "Wash your hands," I ordered.

Mrs. Cardona's eyebrows shot up when Isabella did what I said. "You have experience with *niños?*"

I cocked my head to one side. "Excuse me?"

"With children. You have worked with them before, I think."

"Oh." My cheeks warmed. "Yes. My foster mom in Pittsburgh took in little kids sometimes. And I did a lot of babysitting."

"You have a firm way. Different from most girls your age."

I shrugged. "You want me to set the table?" I asked. "How many places?"

I was hoping and praying that Hector wouldn't come home for lunch. I couldn't imagine sitting around with him and his mother and younger sister for the half hour lunch would take. I couldn't even stand next to him playing a video game without getting overheated, which made no sense because I basically thought he was a jerk.

"Just us three," she said.

Mixed in with my relief was an irritating stab of disappointment. To get over it, I busied myself with setting the table, pouring milk and soda and slicing bread. "It's a big meal for just us girls," I said.

"We Cuban women pride ourselves on our homes and our cooking," she said. "I would never serve Isabella a hot dog in front of the television, like so many American mothers."

Considering that most of my summer lunches had been exactly like that, I guessed I'd been raised wrong. In Mrs. Cardona's eyes, at least.

But what was so bad about hot dogs? Especially when the smell arising from this tamale casserole was, truth to tell, pretty nauseating.

Mrs. Cardona said a short prayer in Spanish and then we dug in. Or they did. Isabella seemed to like the tamale casserole just fine, whereas I occupied myself with moving it around on my plate. Luckily, there was yellow rice and asparagus too, and good bakery bread, so I was in no danger of starving.

"So, is my Hector still running around with that Brianna?" Mrs. Cardona asked out of the blue.

"Uh, well, I don't know," I stammered. My face warmed, and I looked away from her dark, piercing eyes. I had never been a very good liar.

She saw through it instantly. "I thought so," she said, her voice rising. "I told him to stay away from her. Don't have any boys, Alicia. They never listen to their *mamis*."

"Hector gets in a lot of trouble," Isabella volunteered. "*I* not get in trouble."

"I bet," I said. "Mrs. Cardona, I really don't know anything about Hector's social life. We hardly ever see each other at school."

"Hmm." She was obviously stewing. Her own lunch sat untouched on her plate. "He should concentrate on his studies. And his sports. Not girls. Especially not that kind of girl."

I nodded vigorous agreement.

"You don't focus all your attention on boys, do you?"

I swallowed hard so that my Diet Pepsi wouldn't snort out my nose. "Um, no. I'm trying to get a scholarship." I almost said "to go to design school," but I stopped myself in time. I didn't want word to get back to Hector, lest he decide he shouldn't help me beat Brianna.

"That's good." Mrs. Cardona studied me. "Do you ever dress up?" she asked suddenly.

I glanced down at my cargo pants and T-shirt, confused. "What do you mean?"

"I play dress up," Isabella said.

"I mean, you know. High heels, a dress, like that."

"Not very often," I admitted.

"Hector's older sister left some of her clothes behind when she went to college. You should try them on."

"You don't think I dress right?" I asked, hurt. "I make a lot of my own clothes. And all teenagers wear—"

46

She waved her hands, cutting me off with a smile. "I know, I know. I had these discussions with Lucia all the time." She shrugged. "I just hate to see the pretty clothes go to waste. And Lucia, since she went to college, she is a little more, how do I put it—" She waved her hands in the shape of an hourglass.

"She's fat," Isabella supplied.

"No, no, not fat!" Mrs. Cardona slapped her hand. "Talk nice about your *hermana*." She turned to me. "After lunch we will look at the clothes. You try on, maybe take a couple of outfits. They're all designer, all nice."

Though I didn't have high hopes, I wasn't going to turn down an offer like that. I had to be creative with my wardrobe to get through a week without repeating an outfit. And Betsy, nice as she was, had no fashion sense whatsoever. The few shirts and skirts she'd bought me were too droopy and old-fashioned to wear.

So we cleaned up, and then I followed Mrs. Cardona upstairs. After we'd gotten Isabella to play dress up in her own room, Mrs. Cardona threw open a bedroom closet to reveal rows and rows of ironed jeans and color-coded shirts, a stash of frilly church dresses, and box after box of shoes, neatly labeled by color and style.

"See, now, something like this." She pulled a red blouse with a deep v-neck off a hanger and held it up to me. "It would highlight your coloring. You wear too many of these earth tones." She tugged at my beige T-shirt.

A funny feeling curled in my stomach. I really wasn't used to anyone looking at me closely enough to analyze, and it felt good that she'd even noticed my coloring. On the other hand, I'd made my own clothing choices since I was, like, five years old.

"Try it," she urged.

"With jeans," I parried.

"Okay." She flipped through the jeans and came up with a cute boot-cut pair. Then she stood with her hands on her hips, and I realized she thought I was going to get undressed in front of her.

"Um, do you mind?"

"What?" She looked puzzled for a minute and then the light dawned. "Oh, oh, you like the privacy. Okay, sure."

She stepped outside, and I heard her and Isabella singing a song while I slowly undressed and pulled on the tight jeans and red shirt. On an impulse, I opened a box labeled "red slingbacks" and pulled out some three-inch heels.

When I faced the mirror, my face automatically broke into a smile. Mami had it right that time. I did look great in the red. My lips matched, my eyes sparkled, and my skin seemed to glow.

Not only that, I thought, turning to the side, but between the tight jeans and the spike heels, my body was seriously noticeable. Especially the rear view.

There was a knock on the door. "Let us see, let us see."

When I opened it up, Isabella clapped her hands. "You're so pretty!"

Mami nodded approvingly. "Just get some makeup and nail polish."

She backed into Isabella, who was drinking a juice box. Purple stains landed on my stack of beige clothes.

"Oh, *madre de Dios*. I am sorry." She picked up the clothes, and I thought I saw her hiding a smile.

What was that all about?

"I will wash these," she said. "Just leave those clothes on, okay?"

By the time I'd opened my mouth to protest, she was out of earshot. I heard the washer starting, and then she returned. "I have to run out for a couple of hours. Even if Hector comes home, you stay with Isabella, yes? He needs to study."

All of a sudden, I sensed a setup. "I thought you were staying here, getting ready for tomorrow."

"Yes, dear, but I need to shop as well." She patted my hair.

"You want me to stay and babysit with Hector here?"

She nodded. "Don't worry. He is a good boy, but he cannot control Isabella. He won't bother you. He knows you are a nice girl."

"Well . . ."

"Be good for Alicia," she said, blowing Isabella a kiss. And then she was gone, leaving me staring after her in confusion.

How had this happened? Oh, well. Maybe Hector wouldn't come home. Maybe I was just imagining that Mrs. Cardona wanted to set me up with him.

Why would she want to do that? I was just a poor foster kid. If she thought Brianna came from a bad family, look at me: I didn't even have a family.

There was no way Mrs. C would want me with her precious son.

And no way her precious son would be seriously interested in me.

Isabella and I were into our fourth game of Candy Land when a key sounded in the door. "The great one has arrived," came a male voice.

Hector.

And didn't it just figure he'd greet his family like that?

"Your mom's not home," I said when he strutted into the kitchen.

"Hector!" Isabella ran to him, and he swooped her up into his arms. Causing his very significant biceps to bulge nicely.

"What are you doing here?" he asked. His face looked a little red. Maybe he was remembering what he'd called out when he walked in the door.

"Babysitting your sister," I said.

"You've got more patience than I do if you're playing board games with her." He smiled at me.

Why did his approving expression turn me into a marshmallow? *He's taken, he's taken,* I reminded myself.

Since he was occupying Isabella, I took advantage of the moment to collect all the stray Candy Land cards off of the floor. When I straightened up and looked at him, he was staring as if mesmerized.

"What?" I asked.

He shook his head, blinking. "Wow. You look . . . great."

It was my turn to blush. I'd forgotten that I was wearing Latina Princess clothes. The look in Hector's eyes both warmed me and made me angry.

He was obviously much more interested in me now that I was dressed all sexy. But what did that say? These clothes were totally not me.

Besides which, he already had a girlfriend.

"So how's Spanish class going?" He leaned against the counter, studying me.

"Not that you've cared for the last two weeks."

"What's that supposed to mean?"

"It means," I said, "that it takes spike heels and tight jeans to turn you into a concerned friend."

He grinned and shrugged. "So I'm a guy," he said. "We should set up that tutoring."

Isabella tugged at my sleeve. "Mami said I can watch TV when Hector comes home. So he can talk to you. Will you put on *Rugrats*?"

"Please," Hector prompted her.

"Please." She offered a winning grin, identical to his.

Suddenly, I'd had it with the whole Cardona family. "I'm outta here," I said. "Hector, I'm sure you can manage to turn on the TV by yourself."

"But Mami said you should stay." Isabella started to cry.

"Stay," Hector said. "Please. I can tell you're good with kids. I can't deal when she's like this."

51

"Oh, I'm sure one brat can handle another just fine," I said to him, quietly enough that the sobbing Isabella couldn't hear.

Then, as best as my spike heels permitted, I stomped out.

Chapter Six

"Look! It's Alicia Juh-min-ezzz!"

I'd have recognized Ralphie's nasal tone anywhere, but it really sucked hearing it here, at the Linden High open house. It was stressful enough that kids and parents came together, and that Betsy and Ray took it superseriously.

But if I had to put up with Ralphie's mockery as I listened to my teachers struggle to find something good to say about me, I might as well just sink through the floor.

"Alicia's really . . . quiet!" my English teacher had said brightly.

"She's doing solid B work," my math instructor had said, and looked right past us as if to say, "Next!"

My old foster mom would've been proud of Bs. But clearly Betsy and Ray expected better. I could tell from their tight, forced smiles. And I couldn't help remembering the academic awards from their own kids that lined the walls of the downstairs rec room. Spelling

Champ. Best Science Project. Math Award, grades nine, ten, and twelve.

"So, are you having fun yet?" Ralphie asked me.

"Alicia, do you want to introduce us to your friend?"

"No!" I wanted to scream, but I didn't. "This is Ralphie," I said instead. "He's in a couple of classes with me."

"Pleased to meet you," Betsy said. "Are your parents here?"

"Yeah, but they're not hanging out with the likes of me." He gestured toward a designer-clad couple who were talking to the principal.

"Oh, you're Judge Mixon's son?"

"That would be me. Have you heard stories?"

They went on chatting for a few minutes, and I was surprised that Ralphie seemed almost human. Parents had a civilizing influence on high schoolers, I decided. Things weren't quite as cutthroat as usual. The keepers were here, guarding the zoo.

"Oh, look, Alicia! There's your *friend* Hector." Ralphie's voice carried a clear smirk in it.

"Howdy, neighbor!" Ray called across the crowded hallway, and I cringed. Did he have to act so weird in public?

Mrs. Cardona came bustling over. Hector trailed behind her with a resigned expression on his face.

She grabbed my cheeks in her two hands. "Alicia, Alicia," she said with a strong Spanish intonation that I knew Ralphie would delight in imitating. "You are a *bad* girl!"

"Why?" I asked.

She shook her head and gave my cheeks another pat before dropping her hands. "You did not stay long enough to receive your pay. And you left Isabella with Hector, *madre de Dios!* When I arrived home, she had eaten so many cookies, she had no dinner and no sleep!"

"Sorry," I mumbled, and gave Hector a look. "She hadn't had *any* cookies when I left."

Hector threw up his hands. "Cookies were the only thing that kept her from crying. She wanted Alicia. She's crazy about her."

Mami gave him a sideways look. "I think you know more than you are saying about why this poor girl left," she said, putting an arm around me.

"I'm sorry, Mrs. Cardona," I said, because I really wanted to get paid. "Maybe I can babysit for you another time."

"You come over tomorrow, and I will pay you and give you the clothes. And some *bizcochitos*," she said. "You are so skinny."

I saw how Hector's eyes gravitated to my rear end, now dressed in regular, not supertight, jeans. *Doesn't seem to bother your son,* I thought, but didn't say it.

He caught me catching him looking, and his face turned red. "Mom, there's Coach Waters," he said.

"And we still have Alicia's Spanish class to visit," Betsy said. "It was nice to see you."

"*Adios, amigos,*" Ray added with an exaggerated accent that I thought might offend Mrs. Cardona. But she only rolled her eyes and turned away.

As we walked toward my least favorite classroom, Betsy grilled me. "Did you leave your babysitting job early, Alicia?"

"I left after Hector got home."

"Did Mrs. Cardona want you to stay until she came back?"

"That's what she said." I kept my eyes on my fingernails, stroking at a small chip I'd found in the pale pink polish.

"Why didn't you stay, then? It was your responsibility."

"Did it have something to do with Hector?" Ray asked.

"Oh, Ray," Betsy said.

"What? He's a very nice young man, but I wouldn't trust any red-blooded sixteen-year-old with a girl as pretty as Alicia."

I clapped my hands over my ears and shook my hair forward to cover my reddening face. "I'd really love to stop talking about this," I said. "Look, here's my Spanish class."

But walking into the room made my insides jump. It was already the site of a lot of failure, and Mrs. Leaf didn't like me. "Look," I said, "it's a long line, and it's getting late. Maybe we should skip this one last class."

"Oh, no, we couldn't do that," Betsy said.

"We've got to talk to Amanda Leaf," Ray added. "We're old friends of hers. We did a trip to Puerto Vallarta together with sixteen hormonal teenagers. We're bonded for life!"

"You went on a trip with Mrs. Leaf?"

"To Mexico," Betsy said. "It was when John was a junior. Heather was fourteen, and she came with us. It was really fun."

"Well, it was *somewhat* fun," Ray corrected. "And it was somewhat torturous, but what can you expect with a junior class trip?"

"Are your kids really good at Spanish?" I asked wistfully.

"They speak like natives compared to us," Betsy said. "It's so much easier to learn when you're young. They were ordering our meals and asking for directions on that trip."

Oh, great, I thought. Just another example of how well I don't fit into this family.

Minutes later, Mrs. Leaf cried out, "Betsy!" She sounded more animated than she ever sounded in class. "Ray! Oh, how nice to see you." She hugged them and urged them into the chairs in front of her desk. I looked around and realized that everyone else had gone.

"How *are* you?" she gushed, perching on the edge of her desk. "I swear, I never have kids like yours anymore. No one even wants to travel. Too busy working at McDonald's or watching MTV."

I stood off to one side, feeling awkward. There was an extra chair, but I would've had to slide past Mrs. Leaf to get into it, and I didn't feel like it.

Betsy glanced over my way, and that made Mrs. Leaf notice me for the first time. "*Hola,* Alicia," she said in a much cooler voice. "What are you doing here? Where are your parents?"

"Amanda," Betsy said, standing up to put an arm around me, "did you know that Alicia is our foster daughter?"

"What?" Mrs. Leaf looked from me to them in obvious disbelief.

"That's right!" Ray boomed out. "We're glad she has a chance to learn Spanish with you. Just like the old days."

"Well," Mrs. Leaf said, and stopped.

I stared at the floor, studying the patterns that swirled across the tiles.

"You know," she began again, "I did hear something about you taking in a foster child. But I didn't connect—" She broke off again.

I stole a glance up at Betsy and Ray. The happy expressions were starting to fade from their faces.

"Oh, my." Mrs. Leaf walked around her desk to pick up her grade book and a file folder.

"Is there a problem, Amanda?" Betsy asked in her worried voice.

"What problem could there be?" Ray asked. "Alicia's doing pretty well in all of her classes. There's no reason she shouldn't be acing Spanish, of all things."

I cleared my throat. "I'm not doing too well."

Mrs. Leaf flipped through her book and ran her finger down a page. "Actually, she's failing."

Betsy drew in her breath in a shocked gasp.

"Failing?" Ray said as if he'd never before heard the word. Which he probably hadn't. That wasn't part of his enormous vocabulary.

"Yes, failing," Mrs. Leaf said. "She's failed every

quiz and didn't turn in a paper. She hasn't even turned in her homework, and that's an automatic A if you do it."

"What's going on, Alicia?" Ray asked.

"Yes, what's the problem? And why didn't you tell us about it?"

I shrugged. "Spanish is hard for me."

Mrs. Leaf looked skeptical. "That's a little hard to swallow," she said, "considering."

I didn't have to ask, *Considering what?* I already knew. Considering my name. Considering my looks. Considering my heritage.

Betsy's blue eyes were big and round, her voice worried. "Alicia hasn't ever lived with a Spanish-speaking family," she explained. "Well, since . . . since she was quite small."

Since her parents abandoned her, I added mentally.

"There must be something she can do to pass," Ray boomed.

"Something *we* can do," Betsy added. "We want to help."

"How about some kind of extra research project?" Ray suggested. "She could do a report for the class, write a paper, do a Web page, whatever you want."

I fought to keep from crying. Like I didn't have enough to do trying to learn the answers to the simple quizzes I kept flunking.

"That's a possibility," Mrs. Leaf said.

"Could it make up for some of the failing grades?" Ray asked. "Get her to a point where she's passing?"

"That's not unheard of." Mrs. Leaf tapped her pencil on her grade book. "I can work with you on that."

I bit my lip to keep from snapping out something nasty about how she'd never have agreed to such a thing if I'd proposed it myself.

"And what if we found her a tutor?" Betsy asked. "I'm sure there's someone. Maybe you could make a recommendation."

"Of course. I'll look through my records." Mrs. Leaf's voice was getting warmer and warmer as she realized that Betsy and Ray were going to take over her problem.

My heart, on the other hand, was getting colder and colder. The last thing I wanted was to have them all in my business. I could solve this problem myself! In fact, I already was. I didn't need a mommy and daddy doing it for me. I didn't *want* them taking over.

A bell rang, signaling the end of the open house. None too soon for me. I was about to explode, though whether wrath or tears would come out was anyone's guess.

I held it together until we walked out of the high school. Ray and Betsy were quiet too. But when we got to the car, everyone talked at once.

"Alicia, I hope you'll keep us better informed about—"

"I can't wait to sink my teeth into a good research project—"

"I can do it myself!" I shouted.

Ray was opening the car door for Betsy, and both

of them froze. They'd never heard me raise my voice before.

Once I'd started, it was hard to stop. "You talked about me like I wasn't even a person. I was there, you know! I've been sitting in that class while Mrs. Leaf shakes her head and acts like I'm stupid. Maybe she's your old friend, but she clearly hates me!"

"Alicia—"

"I'm taking care of it, okay? I know someone . . . some people . . . who are gonna tutor me."

"But you need a way to make up for what you've already failed," Ray said.

"Fine, I'll do research. But my own research, okay? I don't want you building some Mexican bridge or something!"

Ray's lower lip came out. "How'd you read my mind? I love building bridges!"

"I'm glad you want to try it yourself, Alicia," Betsy said. "But we want you to keep us informed. If you need us, we'll step in. We won't let you fail."

Yeah, because it would reflect badly on you, I thought but didn't say. I climbed into the backseat of the car, knowing what I had to do.

I had to call Hector and set up that first tutoring session as soon as I got home.

Chapter Seven

"Mrs. Cardona?" *Rats.* "Um, it's Alicia. May I speak to Hector, please?"

There was the tiniest silence, into which I read her old-fashioned disapproval: *Girls should not call boys.*

But when she spoke, her voice was warm. "Of course, dear, I'll get him. I think he is talking on that wretched cell phone. At least you have the decency to call his home."

Seconds later, he came to the phone. "Hey." His voice was deep and throaty and, I had to admit, very sexy.

"It's Alicia."

"Mom said."

I took a deep breath. Why was my heart pounding like I'd called to ask him out? This was a business agreement! "Um, I called to set up the tutoring. If you're still willing to do it."

"Sure. Hang on." I heard him close a door. "I've been waiting for you to call," he said in a flirtatious voice.

I leaned back against my pillow and studied the

ceiling, trying not to get sucked in. He was with someone else. And besides, I'd seen how family-centered he was. A guy like him would never really date a foster kid like me.

"Well, listen. I really need the tutoring. Ray and Betsy found out today that I'm flunking Spanish—"

"You're flunking?" He snorted. "Isn't that hard to do in Mrs. Leaf's class?"

"Apparently, it *is* possible," I said, hiding my hurt feelings. "Can you help, or not?"

"Sure, Alicia, I can help," he said. "After dinner sometime this week?"

"Thursday," I said, putting it off for a couple of days. Then some devil made me add, "You're sure Brianna won't mind?"

"Don't worry about her." His voice sounded all serious.

"That's cold! You know I'm not advertising that we're doing this. The whole point was to keep it a secret, right? Except from your mom, to get her off your case?"

"Look, Alicia . . ." He trailed off. "Whatever. Look, can I come over there?" he asked. "It's too . . . nosy over here."

I knew what he was getting at. Brianna wasn't going to call or stop by my house. "Sure. See you here, Thursday."

The next day after school, I headed to the sewing room to work on my dress for the scholarship contest. It had to be done in just six weeks. And since I was about to triple my hours on Spanish, I knew I'd better get in my design time now.

Anyway, designing wasn't work. It was fun and relaxing and creative.

But when I reached the sewing room, my concept of relaxation burst like a kid's bubble.

Brianna.

Man, did she have to be here every time I came in?

I tried to block her out as I headed for my drawer and pulled out the muslin version of my dress. I'd designed it right on the dress form, after the sketchiest of drawings; that was how I liked to work. Most people spent a lot more time working on paper; in fact, I'd had to ask Mrs. Greene if they had a dress form, and then pull it out of storage.

Brianna, of course, had her own dress form at home. Just like she had a drafting table and an up-to-the-minute sewing machine. Whatever her family problems, money wasn't one of them.

Why'd she even need a scholarship, anyway?

I pushed her out of my mind as I carried my muslin dress to the little mirrored dressing room in the corner. This was supposed to be a fun day—I was trying on my dress for the first time—and I didn't want anything to ruin it.

I took off my jeans and shirt and pulled the muslin over my head, working carefully around the pins. I'd just basted a lot of it together, so it was kind of fragile.

Pins pulled out, pricking my sides and arms. As I struggled to slip the dress down over my body, I heard a rip and knew the side seam was coming out.

I reached up, my arms only halfway into the sleeves, and pulled the top part of the dress down over my head so I could see in the mirror. I shook my hair out of the way and stared.

I couldn't believe it! The dress was too small.

Way too small.

I inched the fabric back up my torso and studied my body, naked except for bra and panties. Had I gained weight on Betsy's health-food casseroles?

Once again I tried to slide the dress down over my body.

Rip! The other side seam started to go.

Frustrated, I pulled the dress back off and studied it. I'd designed it for myself because I intended to have myself photographed in it for the competition. You didn't have to do it that way—you could hire a model, but of course I didn't have money to do that. Most of the other contestants didn't, either, and designed their clothes for themselves. Only overweight or camera-shy girls—or boys, there were always a few boys—used models.

So just two weeks ago I'd set the dress form to my exact measurements. Could my body have changed that much in two weeks?

Or had I done the dress form wrong?

I yanked my regular clothes back on, flung open the curtains, and stomped over to the dress form. I grabbed a tape measure and wrapped it around the form's waist.

Twenty-one inches? Yeah, right. I mean, I'm thin. But not that thin!

I measured the hips and the bust. Again, a crucial two to three inches smaller than me.

Could I have made such a big mistake when I was setting up the form?

I felt sick. The difference was just enough that now I couldn't use the muslin. I'd have to start over with new fabric, because my seam allowances weren't big enough for me to let this dress out.

How could I have been so stupid? I never made this kind of mistake! Never in all my years of sewing. So why now, when it was so important?

Now, when I was in direct competition with the bitch of the universe for a prize that meant everything to both of us?

Slowly, I turned around to look at Brianna. She spun back toward her cutting table, but not before I saw the nasty smile on her face.

She'd been watching me measure the form. Watching because . . .

Heat suffused my body as I threw down my tape measure and marched over to her. "You altered my dress form!"

Her eyebrows lifted and her blue eyes opened wide. "What are you talking about?"

Right then, I knew for sure that she'd done it.

"How could you?" I railed at her. "How could you do something so cruel? So unethical?"

"Maybe you just gained weight," she said with a glance at my midsection. "You're looking a little . . . pouchy."

"I didn't gain three inches everywhere in two

weeks!" I threw the dress down. "You're evil. And I'm telling Mrs. Greene what you did."

She laughed. "Like she'd believe you. You can't prove anything."

The fact that she was right made me even more furious. "It's not fair." My hands clenched into fists. "You're rich. You don't even need this scholarship."

She snorted. "If you only knew."

"No," I said. "I'm not gonna feel sorry for you like Katie does. I don't care if you've got it bad at home, you're still a complete witch for doing this to me. You're a cheating, lying, sneaking sack of—"

"Shut up!" Her hands flew to her hips, and she leaned toward me in a threatening stance. "Like you're so much better. You're the wench that's trying to steal my boyfriend. You're the sneaky one."

"What are you talking about?" I asked, but I felt my face turn red.

And Brianna had sharp eyes; she noticed right away. "See? You *are* after Hector. I knew it."

"Knew *what?*" I asked.

"You're wearing those hot jeans and tight shirts he likes. And I know where you got them too: they're from his sister. God, it so sucks that you live right next door to them. Talk about having chances every day . . . and then what you did . . ."

Had she found out about the Spanish lessons? I tried to think even as her sputtering tirade continued. Maybe I should try to smooth things over, develop an explanation. Except if I talked to Brianna at all about the lessons, Hector might refuse to do them. He'd said it didn't matter if she knew, but I didn't believe that for a minute.

So I stood, listening to her rant and wondering how the tables had turned so badly. I had to get back on offense.

"Wait a minute," I said when she paused for breath. "We're getting off the subject of your sabotage. This muslin is my property, and you ruined it!"

"I didn't touch your muslin," she said with a smirk.

And of course she hadn't. She'd altered the dress form, which was school property any student could use.

"Anyway," she said, "maybe I just needed the form for a quick fix to my outfit. Not that I'm admitting I touched it," she added. "But I am a little more . . . *petite* than you are."

I wasn't buying it. And as she launched back into a recitation of all the ways I was ruining her life, I just stood there feeling like a sucker.

I should have been watching my own back. I shouldn't have trusted that the dress form would stay the same size. I should have been more careful!

I would've hauled off and hit her, except I was afraid that hurting Brianna would jeopardize my tutoring relationship with Hector before it even got started. How had she found out about the tutoring, anyway?

". . . and getting access through his brat of a sister and his mean old *mami* . . . That's just rich. Who'd have ever thought the babysitter trick would work?"

"What?" I cocked my head to one side.

"You're such slime. Of course they would never let

me babysit their precious little Cuban princess, but you move in from God knows where and they're leaving her with you like it's nothing! And paying you for it!"

"Wait. You're upset because I babysit Isabella?"

"Well, duh. It's such a . . . a *tactic*."

My breath whooshed out in a sigh of relief. She hadn't found out about the Spanish lessons. I wasn't in danger of losing my ticket to winning the scholarship.

"Whatever, Brianna." I picked up my muslin off the floor and started folding it. I'd have to copy the design in new muslin; that's all.

"You're not just getting away with it. I'm onto you. And I'm not done."

Chapter Eight

That night I was on the phone with Jimmy, moaning about what Brianna had done, when the doorbell rang.

I peeked out the window. "Hector's here!" I said into the phone, and then scrambled down the stairs to get the door before Betsy and Ray did.

"He came over?" Jimmy was asking in my ear. "What for? My God, what are you wearing?"

"For tutoring. Gotta go." I clicked off the phone, glanced down at my new red tee and tight jeans, and tried to calm my fluttering stomach.

Then I opened the door. "Hi," I said. "Thanks for coming."

He looked nice in a button-down shirt with sleeves rolled up to reveal well-muscled forearms, and loose, superfaded jeans. His beard was stubbly. He was such a man already!

Blushing at my thoughts, I nodded toward the staircase. "Let's go up to my room before Betsy and Ray come in. They're out back arguing about some lilac—"

"We're doing this in your bedroom?" he interrupted.

"Uh-huh." I hadn't even thought about it. I always had girlfriends come to my bedroom. The truth was, I'd never had a guy come to my house before, not since I was about eight and the Swaggart twins came over to play with my foster brother and me.

I'd never had a guy come over who was like Hector. Sexy.

Blushing harder, I led the way up the stairs. "I don't want to get tutored in front of my genius parents," I said by way of explanation. "I feel stupid enough already."

"Not for long," he said, waving a sheaf of *Cosmopolitan* magazines. "I brought the good stuff for us to learn from."

"*Cosmo*?" I asked skeptically. I led the way into my room and sat down on the floor, leaning against the bed.

He sat down beside me. "Spanish *Cosmo*," he explained.

"Oh!" I looked at the magazines and registered that the headlines were all in Spanish. " 'La Estrella Más Popular,' " I sounded out.

He laughed. "Say that again."

"What? *La estrella más popular?*"

"You," he said, "have got the worst Spanish accent I've ever heard. Pop—ooo—laaar," he said slowly.

"Oh, fine, make fun of me." I shoved the magazine away. "Aren't teachers supposed to be supportive, not mean?"

"Relax." He patted my leg. "Just relax." His hand

started going in a little circle on my thigh. It wasn't up near the *top* of my thigh or anything. It was more like an unconscious thing on his part.

But not on mine. "Cut it out," I said. My voice sounded breathless.

"What? Oh. Sorry." He yanked back his hand as if he'd touched something hot. "Um, yeah, I shouldn't have laughed. Here." He reached for the stack of magazines and pushed one toward me. "Find something you think looks interesting, and we'll talk about it. In Spanish."

"Yeah, right." I thumbed through the magazine, still catching my breath. My thigh seemed to tingle where he'd touched it. What would it be like to have those big, gentle hands holding me?

And then I shook my head. It was arrogant Hector Cardona I was fantasizing about. Brianna's boyfriend. And anyone who would choose Brianna could have no possible interest in me. Not that I *wanted* someone who couldn't see past Brianna's beauty to her heart of cold, cold ice.

"What's wrong?" Hector asked in a gentle voice.

I opened the magazine blindly to a page and shoved it at him. "Here. What's that about?"

Hector looked startled by my gruff tone, but he took the magazine and studied the page. Red crept up his neck.

"What is it?" I asked.

"Oh, nothing. Let's choose a different story." His whole face was flushed now.

I felt a smile spread across my face. Let him be the

embarrassed one for once. "What's wrong?" I asked. "Is the *Es-pan-yole* too hard for you?"

"Of course not," he snapped.

"Then what does it say?" I scooted closer to look at the picture. It was just a woman in a red dress. Sure, she had a flirty, sexy look about her, but didn't every photo and ad in *Cosmo* use models with that look? "What does that line say?" I asked, pointing to one of the subtitles.

He read it aloud . . . in Spanish.

And can I just say that Spanish, spoken in a low, husky tone by an utterly gorgeous dark-haired muscleman, is pretty amazing? Especially when he says a phrase while looking right into your eyes?

"What's it mean?" I asked softly, meeting his gaze.

He licked his lips. "It means," he said, " 'How to dress . . .' " He broke off, laughed a little, and turned his face away. "I can't say it."

"What?" I squealed, slapping at him, aware that I was acting like the coy, flirtatious girls I despised. "Come on, Hector, tell me!"

"All right, all right!" His voice was rising and he was laughing harder. "It means, 'How to dress so he'll want to take it off.' "

"Oh, my gosh!" I was mortified and laughing at the same time.

Behind us, there was no warning squeak of the bedroom door. Just Ray's voice saying, "And that's not something you should be learning from Hector, Alicia. Or from anyone, for that matter. What is going on in here?"

Hector jumped to his feet, his face a dark scarlet. "I'm sorry, Mr. Dasher. We were just doing some studying—"

"About men taking off women's clothes?" Ray was all the way in the room now, and his customary jokiness was missing.

"Hector's tutoring me in Spanish," I explained. "With Spanish magazines."

"I'm not sure that's the best teaching tool," Ray said, his fisted hands relaxing a little. "And I'm certain that Alicia's bedroom isn't the best learning location."

"I was surprised when she invited me to come up here, but I thought she'd okayed it with you."

I shot Hector a dirty look. Suck-up. "You didn't seem to mind a minute ago."

"Yes, it sounded like a little too much fun was being had in here," Ray said. "How about taking it downstairs, to the kitchen table?"

"But that's so public," I protested.

"Exactly my point."

I sighed and pouted as Hector hastened to gather up the magazines and follow Ray downstairs. I felt like kicking his broad back.

"I didn't have any bad intentions, sir," Hector was saying, as if he really cared what Ray thought. "I'm being neighborly, I guess."

"Uh-huh," Ray said in a dry voice, and held open the door to the kitchen.

We sat down at the table. Ray didn't stay, but I could hear him puttering around in his study next door. A little louder than usual, so I think he was reminding us of his presence.

Not that Hector needed a reminder. He was suddenly all business.

He reached into his pocket and pulled out some cards. "I did bring another teaching tool," he said. "Ooh, big fun: flash cards!"

He held up a brightly colored picture, clearly targeted toward the toddler set. "What is it?"

"It's a house," I said sulkily.

"In *espanol*?"

I shrugged.

"Come on, everyone knows this," he coaxed. "Haven't you ever heard the expression *mi casa es su casa*?"

It just sounded like a big jumble of syllables to me. "No."

"You don't know 'house' in Spanish? Even after the giant hint I just gave you?"

"Shut up!" I said. "I hate Spanish."

He put down the flash cards. "Why do you hate it so much? Is it something in your background?"

I shrugged. "Who knows?"

"Did you ever hear Spanish, growing up?"

I stared down at the table, rubbing my finger over a knot in the wood. "Not since I was three. That's when I was . . . put out . . . into foster care." I had to squeeze the words out past a lump in my throat. I never talked about this stuff.

"Hmm, so you were Isabella's age."

"But I don't remember. Anything."

He tapped his fingers on the table repetitively—*tap,*

tap, tap. "You ever hear this?" he asked suddenly, and started singing:

"Papitas, papitas
Para mamá.
Las quemaditas,
Para papá."

His deep voice and the words of the song brought an odd remembered warmth to my heart. Shutting my eyes, I seemed to feel a man's big hands holding me on his knee, bouncing gently. I felt myself laughing as I looked into warm brown eyes.

Such a rush of love swept through me that it left me breathless.

"Alicia?"

The way he said my name, with its Spanish inflection, made my eyes fly open. My mouth opened too, about to say, "Daddy?"

But of course it wasn't my father. He'd abandoned me when I was a little kid. It was just Hector, looking kind but confused.

Tears sprung to my eyes, and I turned my face away from him quickly. I pushed the flash cards away and stood up. "I'm done."

He stood too, and I felt a hand patting my shoulder. "That must be . . . awful. I can't imagine why your family . . ." He trailed off and put an arm around my shoulders, pulling me sideways toward him.

I took deep breaths and blanked out my mind until

my emotions came under control. After a moment, I looked up. "Don't worry, I won't cry," I told him.

Our eyes caught, and his were full of warmth and compassion. He did care. It felt really, really good.

The thing is, we kept looking. And slowly the feeling between us changed from caring friends to something else. I knew it when his gaze flicked down to my mouth at the same time his arm tightened around my shoulders. It was like he wanted to pull me to him.

A loud bang jolted us apart. "Sorry," Ray called from the next room, where he'd obviously dropped some books. Probably on purpose.

Hector took a couple of steps backward. "I better go."

"Yeah, 'cause you don't have any bad intentions." I felt unreasonably angry at Hector, as if *he* were the one who'd abandoned me. All because he'd sung that stupid song.

I spun around and ran upstairs, ignoring Betsy's concerned questions and Ray's curious face peeking out of his study.

Chapter Nine

The next day, I waited while Katie drooled over cafeteria chocolate cake and strawberry pie. "Oh, should I or shouldn't I?" she agonized.

"We could split a piece of cake," I offered.

Behind us, Jimmy was strategizing. "If we sit one table over from our usual place, we'll be right beside Ralphie Mixon and his friends."

"Perfect!" Katie said. "Oh, but then I don't want cake. I don't want to look like a pig to him. You get it, Alicia, and give me a bite."

"I am *not* sitting anywhere near that little twerp." I put the cake on my tray and walked toward the cashier.

Jimmy swerved gracefully in front of me, paid, and headed for the table he'd selected.

After Katie and I paid, I started in the other direction, but she grabbed my arm and nudged me toward Jimmy. "Come on, help us out," she said.

I stared at her. "You really like him, don't you?"

She shrugged. "I do. And I really, really want a

boyfriend." She lowered her voice and stepped closer. "No one has ever asked me out, or held my hand, or anything."

"But Ralphie?" I asked, even as I followed her toward the table where Jimmy was setting his stuff.

"He's so funny," she said.

"Yeah, except when you're the one he's picking on." I set my tray down and steeled myself for thirty minutes of mockery.

But it didn't happen. He looked our way but didn't call out any insults.

"Talk among yourselves," Jimmy whispered. "Don't stare at him."

"Okay, okay," I said, and I told them about my tutoring session with Hector. I left out the part where I'd gotten all emotional, but kept in the Spanish *Cosmo* and Ray's intrusion. By the time I'd hammed it up, they were both laughing.

"Girl, you were so close to being kissed by the hottest boy in school," Jimmy said.

"I can't believe he brought over *Cosmo*," Katie said. "See, that shows how he's sensitive to girls and what they like."

"Ooh, he's standing up." Jimmy had gone back to watching Ralphie. "He might come over here. Get ready!"

"You guys don't take my problems seriously," I said, only half joking.

Jimmy didn't even bother to look my way. "You've got the hottest guy in school wanting to kiss you. So what's the problem?"

"Yeah," Katie chimed in. "I'm fat and Jimmy's gay. We're the ones who need to go on *The Love Doctor*. From where we sit, your life looks pretty good."

"But he's already got a beautiful girlfriend," I pointed out.

"You're the only one who believes that. You and Brianna."

Mrs. Leaf, my Spanish teacher, crossed the cafeteria between our table and Ralphie's. Seeing her pushed away my hopeful feeling.

"Hi, Mrs. Leaf!" Katie called cheerfully.

"Shut up!" I grabbed Katie's waving hand and pulled it down. "Don't call attention. I'm in trouble with her!"

Too late. She turned our way.

"Thanks so much!" I hissed.

"What? I like her." Katie took a big bite of chocolate cake.

"Me too." Jimmy stopped ogling Ralphie to get in on the discussion. "She's in charge of the school trips abroad, and I want to go next year."

Mrs. Leaf arrived at our table. I was hoping she wanted to talk to Katie or Jimmy, but she zeroed in on me right away. "Alicia, I've been hoping to see you," she said. "It's the last day to sign up for special projects, and I noticed your name isn't on the list."

"Um, yeah."

"Is there a problem?"

There was, but I was embarrassed to admit it. I'd tried to join several of the project groups, but they were full of brainy kids who didn't want to work with a terrible student like me.

"Remember," she said, glancing at Katie and Jimmy, "remember what we talked about at open house."

"I do," I said. Like I could forget. "But all the projects are taken, right?"

"The project that's left is complicated," she said, frowning. "It's on Mexican migrant workers, and there are a lot of social and historical issues involved." She brightened. "Maybe that's a good thing. There's a lot written in English about their situation, so you can do your research that way. But of course you'll need to do a poster and presentation for the fair. In Spanish," she clarified.

"I don't know anything about migrant workers, but I can learn," I said. I hoped my good attitude would give my grade an upward nudge.

"Have you found . . ." She broke off and looked at Katie and Jimmy, who were watching Ralphie and talking. "Would you rather go to the classroom to discuss this?"

I waved off her concern for my privacy. "They know all about it."

"About what?" Jimmy asked.

"That I'm flunking Spanish," I said.

"Now, Alicia, not *flunking*," Mrs. Leaf soothed. It was amazing how much nicer she was to me now that she knew about Betsy and Ray. "Have you found a tutor yet?"

"Um—"

"Yeah, a *hot* tutor," Katie said. "It's Hector Car—"

"No!" I cried out, grabbing her arm. "It's a secret,"

I explained to Mrs. Leaf. "He doesn't want anyone to know. For . . . personal reasons."

"That sweet boy," she said. "He doesn't want to brag about how he helps others. But that gives me an idea."

"What?" I was pretty wary of teachers' bright ideas.

"Hector didn't sign up for a project this year," she said. "Maybe he could work with you on the migrant project. He could help with the presenting, and you could do more of the research."

My heart pounded. The thought of spending hours working with Hector, just the two of us, made me tingle in places I shouldn't. Shouldn't, because he had a girlfriend, even if he didn't mind flirting behind her back. Maybe *because* he didn't mind flirting behind her back. "Well, I don't think—"

"Hector did a report in English about *The Grapes of Wrath* and parallels in today's farm economy," Jimmy offered, grinning at me. "He mentioned migrant workers, I think."

"Perfect!" Mrs. Leaf actually clapped her hands. "I'll go ahead and put you both down."

"But—"

"She'll do it." Katie kicked me under the table. "She'd *love* to. We'll help too."

"Then it's settled." Mrs. Leaf walked away, looking happy.

"Um, guys, hello?" I glared at my friends. "Hector has a girlfriend, who's going to kill me when she finds out."

Lee McClain

"He and Brianna broke up. I'm sure of it." That was Katie, eternally optimistic.

"Besides, you need the grade to get the scholarship, right?" Jimmy patted my arm. "This is good news, Alicia. Just appreciate it."

The truth was, I was scared to death. Scared of what would happen if Hector said no, and even more scared of what would happen if he said yes.

Chapter Ten

I found out soon enough how Hector felt about us working together.

Can you say *ambivalent?*

He came up to me as I slammed my locker at the end of the day. His eyes were darker than usual, and his handsome mouth twisted into a frown. "Do you know what you're doing?"

"About what?" I asked, pretending ignorance to buy time.

"Signing us up for a Spanish project," he said. He stood close enough that I felt heat radiating from his body. A spicy smell—it must have been his aftershave—gave me a strange urge to bury my face in his neck.

"Would it really be so awful to work with me?" I asked in a husky voice that seemed to come from a new part of me.

He inhaled like he was going to say something, then paused with his eyes on my face.

"Would it be totally, totally terrible?" That new girl inside me quirked my lips into a smile.

Hector responded with a smile of his own. One that came and went quickly, like lightning. "No. And that's the problem."

"What is?"

He gazed into my eyes for a moment longer and then slammed his hand against a locker. "Come on. Let's get out of here."

"Are you offering to walk me home?"

He fell into step beside me. "Seeing as how we live next door, I guess I am."

I stood by the exit door, performing the gentleman test. Would he open the door for me or stand there like a dolt?

Naturally, he passed, reaching around me to push open the heavy door, then waiting while I walked through ahead of him. I bet he opened car doors for girls too. Mami had trained him right.

"So what's the problem?" I asked as we walked.

"I'm kinda confused," he said, grabbing a stick and swishing it aimlessly against the bushes and sidewalk. "I was getting vibes like you didn't want to be with me, but this changes things."

"It was Mrs. Leaf's idea!" I wasn't a home wrecker. I didn't want to steal Hector away from Brianna. Well, I sort of did, but I knew it would be wrong. And if he could be so easily swayed to cheat on her, he wasn't much of a prize.

"Even if it was her idea, you could've said no. But you didn't."

"Right, I didn't," I said as we approached my house. "I need the grade to pass Spanish, so I'm doing the project. But if I have to do it alone, I will."

I ran inside before he had a chance to answer. The truth was, I didn't want to hear his final rejection.

Inside, I got online, checked my e-mail, and IMd with Katie a little while. Then she had to go do homework, and I should've too, but I lingered, surfing the Net.

I justified my computer time by looking up migrant workers, and came upon some stuff about Mexico, border crossing, illegal immigrants, and so on. It all sounded like a pretty miserable life, and I hated the thought of spending time researching it. Hunger, poverty, working in fields that didn't even have Porta-Johns . . . I'm sorry, but that was *not* the kind of life I wanted to read more about!

I started to shut off the computer. But some curious, nudging part of me wouldn't allow it. Instead, it guided my fingers to type the address my social worker had given me: *www.altlives.com.*

Instantly a scene came up on the screen, but it wasn't what I expected. Instead of watching farming like before, I saw a small, very plain kitchen with a woman at the stove.

A woman with curly black hair tied back into a long ponytail, light brown skin, and a turned-up nose just like mine.

Her lips were moving, and I knew instantly that she was singing. I could almost hear the soft, crooning song in a voice lower than you'd expect from a woman. Just like I could almost smell the spicy beans she was cooking.

I felt tears running down my face.

The woman spun around from the stove, a smile lighting up her eyes and mouth as two kids ran in and started hugging her. They looked to be maybe eleven and nine. She spent a long moment returning their hugs, then looked at their hands, frowned, and gestured toward the sink.

As the kids went over to wash their hands, I sat limp, almost unable to believe what I was seeing.

This was my birth mom, all right. And apparently she had two other kids. Kids she'd kept.

She'd thrown me away, and then had more kids she'd apparently liked better.

Hot rage brought a flush to my face, and I brushed away my tears. She wasn't worth crying about!

She spun to the door again, and if her face had lit up before, now it was brighter than the sun.

Two men came into the picture. One, I knew automatically, was my father. He had black hair, a little long and a little unkempt, threaded through with white. He walked with a slight limp, and he looked tired. But from the way my mother hugged him, I could tell they were still in love.

The other man, I saw now, wasn't really a man, but a teenager just a couple of years older than me. He wore thick glasses taped together at the temple. He seemed to be waiting patiently for his turn to hug my mother.

One of the younger kids came over, tapped his legs,

and started gesturing with his hands. The older boy leaned close to see. Then he gestured back.

The older man and woman—my parents!—turned toward the teenager, and the father said something, gesturing at the same time.

The teenage boy gestured back, and then the mother enfolded him in her arms.

All of a sudden I understood. This older boy had to be my older brother. And he was deaf. From the looks of things, he didn't see too well either.

My heart thudded in my chest with a dull, heavy pounding that felt like I was about to have a heart attack. I must have known this boy up until I was three. I must have played with him. My older brother. I wondered if he had treated me the way Hector treated Isabella.

This group, this happy, loving family, was *my* family. They lived together, ate together, talked together, sang together. Now they were all helping to set the table and carry food to it. Not much food—just the pot of beans and half a loaf of bread—and they were all drinking glasses of water.

But they were together, a family. And for some reason I didn't understand, they'd abandoned me. Kicked me out. Excluded me from their circle.

My stomach churned as I watched them all bow their heads and pray. The hypocrites! Didn't God know that beneath their loving good manners, they'd coldly discarded another human being, leaving her to be raised by strangers?

The mother dipped out small servings for everyone,

scraping the pot to get a last few beans for herself. Then they all started to eat hungrily. The meal took about two minutes to complete.

The younger boy held out his plate for more. The mother picked up her piece of bread—dry, no butter—and held it toward him. But the father must have said something sharp, because the boy pulled back his hand, looking ashamed.

The mother and father spoke to each other, and for the first time I saw discord within the group. She seemed to be yelling at him, but it was over as soon as it started, and they were all smiling and clasping one another's hands.

It made me sick! I fumbled for the mouse and shut off the computer.

What had I just seen? A poor family who adored one another. A mother who wanted to give her last crust of bread to her child.

To one of her children, anyway. But not to me.

Chapter Eleven

"I can't believe you're making a new dress for a party the day after tomorrow," Katie said two days later as we walked into Colyer's Crafts and Fabric.

I just shrugged. I needed something to distract me from obsessing about my birth family.

"Yeah," added Jimmy, "and not just any party. The party of the year. Lisa Dean is totally popular."

"Makes me wonder why *we're* invited," Katie said.

"Oh, stop," I said. "Everybody loves you."

"And me," Jimmy said, preening.

"No, everybody thinks you're funny," Katie said.

"Even better. Who wants to be Winnie the Pooh?"

"I know, I'm fat." Katie brushed her hands down over her stomach.

"That is *not* what I meant, girlfriend! I just meant everyone loves you like . . . Oh, forget it." Jimmy put an arm around Katie's shoulders. "You're pleasantly plump, that's all."

I ran my hands over some fabric, trying to lose myself in the feel of the material, the smells of fiber, and the clicking, busy sounds of the store. Trying to let them fill the big empty hole in me where the love of my family should have been.

"Aren't you the space case," Jimmy said, and I realized they'd been trying to get my attention.

"Let's look at patterns," Katie suggested with a meaningful glance at me and then Jimmy. They could tell I was upset, but I hadn't told them why. I mean, how do you explain to your friends that you saw your birth family on some magic computer game?

I kept studying some black taffeta with a crinkled texture. "I don't think I want a pattern. I have my dress in mind."

"What's it like?" Jimmy asked, obviously trying to jolly me up.

"Something like this." I pulled out enough fabric to wrap around me in a tight sheath. Then I gestured for his belt. "Take that off."

"Oooh, stripping down in the middle of Colyer's," he said, laughing, but he did it.

I wrapped it around me to form a cinched waistline. "Then a plunging back and slightly poofed skirt."

"But tight at the top, right?" Katie asked wistfully. She longed to wear form-fitting clothes, but they didn't suit her figure.

"Right."

"I love it," Jimmy said, clapping.

A loud harrumph and tapping heels warned us of an approaching adult. "You young people aren't to play with the fabric," scolded a skinny woman with short, severe hair.

"We're not playing with it," Jimmy said as he re-claimed his belt and started to put it on. "She's buy-ing it."

"Yeah, I'm buying it," I decided, and suddenly I felt better. That's what designing did for me. I loved to use my eyes, my fingers, and my imagination to come up with something completely new and different to wear, something I'd never see echoed in the halls of Linden High or anywhere else. I knew this dress would change some in the sewing, but that was part of the fun too.

As I carried the bolt of fabric up to the counter, Jimmy and Katie argued behind me. Since they were always arguing, I didn't pay attention. But as I stood waiting for the crabby lady to measure and cut my fabric, I realized they were arguing about me.

"What?" I asked as they came closer.

"You tell her."

"You."

"What?" I repeated, getting annoyed.

"Okay, I'll do the dirty work, like always," Jimmy said. "You should enter this dress in the competition. Not the one you're making at school."

I shook my head and rolled my eyes. "This is just a throw-together," I said. "It's a bit dramatic for IIFD."

Katie put her hand on my arm. "It's just that your other dress is too much like every other dress they'll see," she said. "This is much more creative."

"But Mrs. Greene said they like classic," I argued.

"Classic, but not identical to everyone else's," Jimmy said. "Your muslin—the one that got ruined—was almost exactly like Brianna's."

"You're not as likely to win with it," Katie said gently.

All of a sudden I got suspicious. "How long have you been thinking my competition dress was lame?"

They looked at each other guiltily.

"How long?"

"Um, basically since you started."

"Why didn't you tell me?"

Katie shrugged. "You were too far along," she said. "But now that you're starting over, you should do this dress."

"You have a chance with this one." Jimmy started to push up to sit on the counter, until a glare from the bitchy fabric cutter stopped him.

"So in other words, Brianna did me a favor? By trashing my dress?"

Katie giggled. "Yes, but don't let her know it," she said. "She'll be at Lisa Dean's party, and if she thinks you're doing anything right, she'll be ready to kill you."

Two days later I remembered Katie's words as I walked into Lisa Dean's party, only to be greeted by an icy glare from Brianna.

The party was loud with music and voices. Even though Lisa Dean's house was huge, it seemed crowded because most people were jammed into the kitchen and dining room. That made it hot. I was glad for my lightweight dress, but regretted the knee-high boots I'd worn with it.

They did look cute, though, and so did the dress. I'd sewed in a mad frenzy for the past two days and had only finished it hours before. The work had kept me from thinking too much about my birth family, and somehow, as I'd cut and basted and hemmed, I'd sewed myself back up again.

It looked pretty bad that my birth family was this loving, wonderful group of folks, and yet they'd abandoned me. Looked bad for *me*, that is. I'd rather have discovered that they were obnoxious, hard-drinking, irresponsible jerks.

But they weren't: they seemed great, and that meant there must have been something wrong with my three-year-old self that made them want to ditch me. I thought of Isabella, bossy and refusing to share, and wondered if that had been the damning factor in my case. Had I cried too much for the last crust of bread? Eaten too much? Been mean to my handi-capped brother?

Whatever it was, though, I knew I'd grown up into a decent person. My foster mom had taught me generosity by example, and she'd drummed into me that I had to be nice to all kinds of kids. My birth family shouldn't have given up on me so soon. If they didn't like how I acted, they should have taught me better.

It might be partly my fault, but not all. Some of the blame had to rest on them.

I caught a glimpse of Hector, perched on a bar stool by himself, and my heart did a weird racing thing in my chest. He looked pensive, in need of comfort. I'd have loved to go over and talk to him, but he hadn't contacted me since the day he'd walked me home from school. I knew we had to talk soon about the project, but a party wasn't the right place to do that.

"I can't believe he brought Brianna," said a voice in my ear, and I turned to see Jimmy staring in Hector's direction.

"Didn't you hear?" asked Katie on my other side. "She totally guilted him into it. Told him he'd ruined her life and her reputation by breaking up with her. He agreed to bring her as a friend."

"Yeah, right. If you believe that, I have a bridge I'd like to sell you." The truth was, I felt like crap learning that Hector had brought Brianna to the party. Not surprised, because I'd known they were still secretly together, but miserable because of the reminder.

Katie said something, but the party's noise drowned it out.

"What?" I asked.

"Come on." Katie pulled me toward the back door, where a cooler full of sodas, beers, and other alcohol told me what I'd suspected the minute I walked in: Lisa's parents weren't here.

My hand hovered over a wine cooler. I'd snuck them before with Champ, my foster brother, and I knew I liked them.

But Betsy and Ray had talked to me about drinking and drugs a couple of times, including two days before when I'd let them know I was invited to a big party, the first one since I'd been in town.

"We know you'll have temptations," Betsy had said in her earnest way. "But we think drinking and drugs are really dangerous for teens. We want you to say no."

"Say no way," Ray had added. "And call us if there's drinking at a party where you are. We'll come and get you, no questions asked."

"Don't even stay at a party where there's drinking or especially where there are drugs," Betsy had said. "Too many dangerous things can happen. Kids lose their judgment."

I'd nodded and promised and tried to get out of there ASAP. Now I thought about their attitude and knew they'd be sniffing my breath when I got home.

No way would I call them to take me home from the party; I wanted to show off my dress, after all.

And to tell the truth, I wanted to see Hector in a social setting—some sick curiosity on my part to see what his relationship with Brianna was like.

I grabbed a Diet Sprite and headed back inside. Katie did the same, and Jimmy took a Mike's Hard Lemonade. It sure felt good to have some friends already, especially at a party like this.

When we got inside, things went downhill fast. First I noticed Brianna standing in the middle of a bunch of girls, crying and talking. They were all petting and consoling her. Poor little tiger! She kept shooting venomous glances at Hector.

Until she saw me, that is. Then *I* became the target.

Brianna talked faster and louder, and the girls with her started staring at me too.

"Am I imagining it, or are they about to lynch me?" I asked Jimmy out of the side of my mouth.

"You're not imagining it. Looks like a war strategy meeting to me." He moved to block my view of the girls. "Come on, there's got to be something else going on at this party."

"There is," Katie said, her eyes widening.

We both looked in the same direction she was, and saw Hector stand up.

I got a tiny hope he was going to come over and talk to me, but then I saw him take a deep breath and head Brianna's way. He said something to the other girls with a tiny little smile, and they all fell away like synchronized swimmers.

Then he started talking to Brianna in a low, intense voice.

"What are they fighting about, anyway?" I had the feeling it was me, but maybe I was just being paranoid. I could almost hear my first foster mom's voice reminding me I wasn't the center of the universe.

"Don't act all innocent," said a girl behind me. "Nice move, making it so you're doing this big school project with Brianna's boyfriend."

I turned to look at her as she smirked and walked away.

Huh. So Hector *was* doing the Spanish project with me. And everyone knew it, and that's why the happy couple was fighting?

"That doesn't make sense," Katie said. "He already broke up with her. Unless *she's* looking for a way to make it look like she's breaking up with him. Oh, my gosh!"

I turned to see what Katie was looking at.

Brianna had drawn back her hand like she was going to slap Hector. It seemed like everyone at the party took one collective breath.

But he caught her wrist easily as she aimed for his face. She pulled away, making like he had hurt her, and said something low and harsh.

He raised his eyebrows and his eyes burned with offense. He turned and stalked over to stand against the bar.

"Come on, show's over. Let's do something else," Jimmy said. "Wonder if Ralphie's here."

I rolled my eyes. "You go ahead and look for him. I'm hungry." And I crossed the room to the table of chips and pizza, which happened to be very close to the bar—and to Hector.

Chapter Twelve

I stood against the wall, eating pizza and thinking about the pros and cons of walking over to Hector and starting a conversation.

He slumped against the wall, alone. I felt bad for him; he'd been shamed in public by the person who was supposed to stand at his side.

At the same time, if I approached him, Brianna's hit squad might very well go after me. If not Brianna herself.

But I didn't like giving a few mean girls control over what I did. Besides, I was feeling a little bit reckless. What did I have to lose, really? I mean, Hector and I *were* friends and neighbors. He was tutoring me, supposedly, and tonight I'd learned we were doing the Spanish project together after all. What could be wrong with a little friendly conversation?

I wiped my hands, pressed my soda can against my cheek to cool down, and took a step in Hector's direction.

His head shot up, but he wasn't looking at me.

Lee McClain

He was watching Brianna as she talked to another boy, her head tilted very close to his. Hector's eyes narrowed like he was waiting for something.

I turned to watch Brianna too. Somehow it was like seeing a car accident in slow motion. I wanted to yell at her to put on the brakes, but of course I didn't.

I didn't even like the girl. Why should I care if she crashed and burned?

I looked over at Hector in time to see his fists clench. Then I looked back at Brianna.

She was kissing the other boy, a long, slow, movie-style kiss.

The party got quiet. Everyone in the room was tennis-matching it like I was: looking at Brianna, looking at Hector. Brianna, Hector.

Even she was doing it. She finally finished the kiss, and instead of looking at the boy—who, lucky for him, happened to be a football player and built like one—she looked at Hector.

So did everyone else, including me. What would he do?

He didn't spare a glance for any of us spectators. Instead he stood, very slowly, his eyes on Brianna. There was a sort of collective gasp in the room, and I heard a couple of guys somewhere behind me say, "Fight!"

Then Hector turned and walked over to me. Like he'd known where I was and been planning this the whole time.

I stood stuck on the spot like a bug on a pin, waiting, squirming, aware of everyone watching me.

He stopped two feet in front of me, just a little too close, and my heart pounded heavy and fast.

"Want to dance?" he asked into the room's silence.

Immediately twenty different thoughts flashed through my mind like subliminal messages on a TV commercial. Thoughts like:

Everyone in this entire room is looking at us.
Everyone will keep on looking at us if we dance.
Brianna will claw my eyes out for this one.
Why didn't he ask me to dance before if he wanted to?

What came out of my mouth was, "No way! You're just using me to get back at her."

I swear there was a little sucking sound in the room, as if everyone inhaled at once.

Hector gave a slow, deliberate look around, a what-are-*you*-looking-at glare.

Then he crossed his arms over his chest and waited.

Finally, little pockets of conversation started up and people at least pretended they weren't listening to every word we said.

Which wasn't much, on his part, so I repeated my accusation. "You're using me. Forget it!"

"I'm not using you. I really do like you," he said.

"Then how come you didn't ask me to dance until Brianna started kissing somebody else?"

He shrugged. "I wasn't in the mood before, but now I am."

"Yeah, to piss her off. Forget it."

103

"It's not to piss her off," he said. He leaned closer to me. "You know I've liked you all along. I thought you felt the same." He locked me with his warm brown-eyed gaze.

All of a sudden I was hot. I couldn't think of what to say.

"Besides," he said a little bit louder, glancing back at Brianna, "I don't date girls like her."

Another hush fell over the room. My stomach twisted as I looked at Brianna's stricken face. Obviously this scene hadn't played out the way she'd wanted it to. I knew instinctively that she had no more interest in the football player bristling by her side than she had in the upholstered chair she leaned on.

She'd just wanted to make Hector jealous. Because *she* was jealous. Of me.

And apparently she was right to be jealous.

"Well, what do you say?" Hector asked. "Want to dance?"

To get my hands on those brawny shoulders, to be held in his strong arms? To see what he smelled like up close?

You bet I wanted to dance. But my pride wouldn't let me be second choice. And besides, I couldn't stop my new, odd identification with Brianna.

"No, thanks," I said, and turned away.

"Why not?"

I looked back over my shoulder at him and at the roomful of people pretending not to listen. "Because I don't dance with boys like you."

* * *

Half an hour later I sat alone on the side porch of Lisa Dean's house, thinking about going home. Being right was damn lonely.

If I leaned to one side and looked through the window, I could see Hector dancing with all the other girls, looking like he was having a wonderful time.

If I looked out into the backyard, I could see Jimmy and a couple of other boys laughing and talking. Ralphie was there too, looking all shy and sweet. Did this mean Jimmy had won the bet?

Meanwhile, here I was all alone. Not fitting in. Not belonging. And it made me wonder if I'd *ever* feel like I belonged somewhere.

For a long time, I'd dreamed about going to design school and creating my own line of clothes. I'd always thought that in the design industry I'd find other people like me, people who loved color and fabric and art. I'd imagined a warm, fuzzy community.

But what if the design world was full of cutthroat witches like Brianna?

I tried to shake off my gloomy mood, but it wouldn't go, and I had to face the reason why. Even more than my design dreams, I'd hoped somewhere deep inside that I could find my birth family and that they would want me back. I'd hoped I'd learn that it was all a horrible mistake or accident, my being abandoned at age three. I'd even imagined tragic fates for my birth parents: maybe they had been fatally ill and had given me away in a last act of love.

Seeing them all healthy and happy and loving—loving with everyone but me, that is—had pretty much crushed me. They looked to be a great family, the family of my dreams. Except they didn't want me.

I didn't belong with my birth family any more than I belonged at this party. My eyes started to well up, and it was only my fear of mascara overflow that kept me from breaking down in tears.

The door from the house burst open.

"Leave me alone!" cried a familiar bitchy voice.

Then the door slammed shut. The light was dim out here, but I was pretty sure who'd joined me on the porch.

"Brianna?" I asked, not wanting her to be surprised into violence by my presence.

"Oh, God, of all the people I don't want to see."

"Go ahead and leave, then. I was here first."

"I can't," she said, flopping down onto a glider. "Everyone's looking at me."

"I thought you liked that."

"Not when they're looking because they think I'm pathetic." She turned sideways and plopped her feet up, either not aware or not caring about the streaks her spike heels left on the cushions. "And don't *you* look at me, either," she snapped in my direction. "Miss Priss."

"What's that supposed to mean?"

Her voice grew mocking. " 'I don't dance with boys like you.' "

"God, shut up!" I started to stand up, then sank back down. I didn't have anywhere to go.

"Easy for you to blow off Hector," she said in a bitter voice. "You have everything."

I squinted at her in the gathering darkness. "You have got to be kidding."

"No, why?"

"*You* have everything. You live in the town where you were born. You have parents, money, your own dress form, a ton of friends—"

"Not friends. People who are scared of me," she corrected. "You came here out of nowhere, and everybody likes you."

I shook my head. "I don't know where you get your information." But I *did* have friends, I realized. Jimmy and Katie definitely had my back. At least when they weren't chasing Ralphie.

"You have parents too, nice parents." She wrapped her arms around her knees. "And you got Hector's interest without, you know, *doing* him."

I blushed, as much for what that comment said about her as what it said, or didn't say, about me.

She shook her head. "I don't know how you did that. How you came here and just, like, eclipsed me. In your ugly clothes, no less."

I'd had enough. "I have foster parents, not real ones. Foster parents who think I'm an idiot, and who could put me out at any minute like my last one did." Which wasn't exactly fair: I'd learned a week ago that my old foster mom needed surgery and wouldn't be able to do foster care anymore, even when she recovered. Not her fault, but I still felt somehow betrayed.

Brianna tapped a cigarette out of a pack in her purse, ignoring me.

Lee McClain

"And I don't have Hector. He's just using me to get back at you."

She lit her cigarette and looked at me with her cool, blank blue stare.

"So don't act like you're all pitiful and I'm not." Suddenly I didn't know what I was arguing for. Was my point that I was more pitiful than her? "And I hate smoking, so I'm outta here." I stormed out into the yard, letting the screen door bang behind me. To hell with waiting for my so-called friends. I'd walk home.

Alone.

As usual.

Chapter Thirteen

Two nights later I pounded hard on Hector's door. Not because I had an urgent message, but because I was still mad at him. I didn't want to go over there, but I had no choice.

"Alicia!" Isabella let me in. Her joyful greeting was accompanied by what sounded like a growl coming from the living room.

"Hector is in a mood," Isabella informed me as she pointed me toward the living room.

"Me, too," I said. If I hadn't needed his help to complete our research project, I would have been tempted to brain him with the pile of books in my arms.

He'd been totally snippy on the phone, acting like he was doing me a huge favor by agreeing to meet. But I was determined. I wanted to get the project done, pass Spanish, and ride the scholarship bus straight over to Europe and IIFD.

Then I'd never have to see Hector, Brianna, or any of the Linden High crowd again.

"Could you turn off the TV?" I asked.

"No," he said without looking at me.

"Look, you did agree—"

"Check it out," he interrupted. "It's about migrants."

I glanced at the screen, then looked harder as I saw a landscape almost exactly like the one I'd seen on the Altlives game. My heart stuttered, and I covered my reaction with sarcasm. "It figures you'd rent a movie instead of doing research."

"When did you turn into Saint Scholastica?" He fumbled for the pause button and hit it. "It's a documentary. Critically acclaimed. I do have some sense of responsibility, even if . . ." He broke off and started studying the spines of the books I'd dumped onto the coffee table in front of him.

"Even if what?" He was acting strange.

"Even if you're playing with me. Or *playing* me."

"What's that supposed to mean?"

"I thought you liked me, at least a little, and then you're all 'no way' when I ask you to dance."

"I told you, I don't like being the backup. I didn't want to be your security blanket to dance with after Brianna got it on with that football player."

"I didn't mean it as an insult, Alicia. Brianna and I were finished a long time ago."

My name sounded sexy in his mouth, and my cheeks heated.

"You were not."

"We were. Right after you came to town, in fact. I just don't broadcast my business the way some people do. Besides," he went on, "none of the other girls seemed to mind dancing with me."

Was he telling the truth? "Yeah, I noticed you certainly made the rounds."

"Did that bother you?" Something sparkled in his rich coffee-colored eyes.

"No! But it bothered Brianna. Which I assume was your goal. Are you back with her yet?"

"Do you care?" He was still looking at me with that little light in his eyes, holding my gaze, obviously trying to read me.

"Why would I? She acts like your owner whether she's with you or not. And she acts like I'm the thief trying to steal her little pet puppy."

"I'm no puppy, I'm a big dog." He grinned at me. "And I'm not back with her."

"You drove her to the party," I muttered, even though I knew I should drop it. "And she's always hanging on you."

He looked right into my eyes. "She begged me not to tell anyone I broke up with her," he said, "and she begged me for a ride to the party. I have a soft heart for an ex-girlfriend. But I won't make that mistake again."

That warmed my heart in the most absurd way. I fought off a big smile. "Let's get to work," I said, grabbing the remote. "What's this documentary about, anyway?"

Pretty soon, the conditions we were seeing pushed flirtation with Hector right out of my mind. We saw kids younger than we were working twelve-hour days, homes without indoor plumbing, and bosses who fired workers the first day they or their kids got sick.

Hector was flat-out appalled. "How can they live like that?" he kept asking, shaking his head.

I was distressed too. I'd known plenty of poor people in my old neighborhood. But it was a different kind of poor. In the city, people might not have food, but they had running water. They might have to leave their kids unsupervised while they worked a night shift at some store or factory, but there were laws that prevented anyone from putting kids to work at age ten.

It upset me to see how similar it looked to Altlives. My birth family's trailer home, their scanty meal of beans and bread, and their worn-out clothes looked a lot like the families on the show.

Were my birth parents migrant workers?

That line of thinking was uncomfortable enough that I was glad Isabella interrupted us. She looked adorable in her Barbie nightgown, her damp hair curling around her face.

"Tía Julia gave me my bath," she announced, flinging herself into my lap. "Now we can play!"

"Just five minutes, then bed, Bella," warned Tía Julia as she sank down onto the couch beside Hector. "The child exhausts me. I'm glad I'm only staying a week. What are you watching?"

"It's a documentary about migrant workers," Hector explained.

Tía Julia studied the screen and then spat out a sentence in Spanish that ended with the word "Mexico."

"No, no," Hector said and then added a long stream of Spanish words.

I didn't understand much of what either of them

had said. I'd actually gotten to where I could understand some Spanish, but not when they talked fast
and angry, like now.

At least I didn't freak out anymore when I heard
Spanish. That was an improvement right there.

Isabella played with my hair while I watched the
screen. I wanted to pause it. The show was interesting. But like all males, Hector had taken control of the
remote, and he was too busy arguing with Tía Julia to
notice the show was passing us by.

"They're talking mean," Isabella said to me.

"Sounds like it," I agreed.

"What's wrong with people from Mexico?" she
asked, attempting to squeeze my thick hair into a
doll-size ponytail holder.

"Ow! Be gentle!" I untangled my hair and handed
her a brush. "Look, just brush it, okay? There's nothing wrong with people from Mexico."

"Tía Julia thinks they're lazy." Isabella got bored
with styling my hair and stood on the couch. "Lazy,
lazy, lazy," she said, jumping up and down. "People
from Mexico are lazy!"

"Hey!" I stood up, grabbed her around the waist,
and lifted her down to the floor. "No jumping on the
couch. And no talking bad about Mexicans. I'm Mexican, and I'm not lazy!"

Silence.

I looked around.

Hector must have finally hit the pause button, because the screen was frozen and both he and Tía Julia
were looking at me.

113

"What?" I asked.

"You were yelling," Hector said.

"Well, look what prejudices you're teaching your sister."

"*I'm* not teaching her anything," Hector said.

"She was just jumping up and down singing that Mexicans are lazy."

Tía Julia went off in Spanish.

"*Entiendes?*" Hector asked me.

I shook my head. "And it's not because I'm lazy, either. It's because I'm blocked. My birth family was Mexican, and they abandoned me, and I've had a block against Spanish ever since."

It was the first time I'd ever said this aloud, and I felt almost as surprised as Hector looked.

"Tía wasn't saying all Mexicans are lazy," he said, looking over at his aunt. "She was talking about . . . certain ones. Like those on this show."

I pointed to the frozen picture on the screen. It showed a row of men on their knees, picking some sort of vegetable by hand. "Do they look lazy?" I asked her.

She said something else in Spanish, rapidly, obviously trying to explain herself.

"*En Ingles, por favor,*" Hector said. "You're probably right, they're ignorant, but it's not their fault. They have no education and no opportunities."

"They should work to improve themselves," Tía Julia said.

"Sure, everyone should," Hector agreed.

"What should they do?" I asked. I walked over to

Hector and grabbed the remote, hit play, and turned off the sound. We could all see the men bent over, harvesting some crop at a rapid pace. "Should they say, 'Excuse me, Boss, I need the afternoon off to go to college'?"

"I meant no offense," Tía said quietly. "I didn't realize you were Mexican."

Not only Mexican, but a migrant worker by birth, I thought. Somehow I knew it was the truth. Everything from the documentary was just too similar to what I'd seen on my computer. My birth family lived in identical circumstances. Their trailer home was strangely bare, without the personal touches it would have if they lived there full time.

Mami walked into the room. "What's going on in here? I heard shouting. Isabella, you should be in bed."

"Alicia's trying to turn me and Tía Julia into bleeding-heart liberals," Hector said. "Trying to make us agree that migrant workers can't help it that they're bad off."

"Well, can they?" Mami asked mildly as she picked up Isabella's hairbrush and started stroking her sleepy daughter's hair.

"We worked our way up," Tía Julia said.

"That's true," Hector agreed. "Our family wasn't well off to begin with, and we worked hard to get where we are."

"What do you know about hard work?" Mami said. "I pick up your clothes and wet towels every day."

I had to laugh at the image of Hector dropping his clothes where he stood, confident that his mother would clean up after him.

"You better work on that if you want to find a wife someday," Tía Julia scolded him. "Modern girls aren't slaves to their men. Right, Alicia?"

"Right."

"*I* put my clothes in the hamper better than Hector," Isabella announced, then gave a huge yawn.

We all laughed, even Hector. And he looked at me with such warmth that I felt it from my toes to my heart.

"Don't let his tough talk fool you," Mami said to me. "My Hector has a heart for the downtrodden, always has." She ruffled his hair as if he were a little boy.

As Tía Julia and Mami led Isabella out of the room, mixed feelings surged up inside me.

I loved the sense of belonging to this family, of being able to argue politics one minute and laugh together the next. I loved how close they all were, how Tía Julia came and stayed for a week even though she only lived an hour away, how Isabella could go to any of them with her three-year-old problems and be completely certain of getting the help she needed.

But this wasn't the kind of family I'd been born to. I wouldn't have had a Barbie nightgown and a bubble bath every night. I wouldn't have even had enough to eat. And by age ten or twelve, I'd probably have been working full-time in the fields.

Only to be scorned by families like the Cardonas, scorned for not improving my life.

"Don't let Tía Julia bother you," Hector said, coming to sit beside me on the couch. "She doesn't read or think about things the way Mami does. She just talks about her opinions."

I shrugged. "It's okay." I didn't want to tell him that the person whose opinions really bothered me was him, not Tía Julia.

Hector definitely had more sympathy for the migrant workers than his aunt did. But still he felt himself way above them, like he was a better person. Smarter and harder-working. He couldn't imagine himself ever leading a life like theirs.

I didn't think he'd be sitting so close to a migrant worker on the couch, either. He'd probably find her too smelly and dirty and ignorant.

It was just an accident of fate that made me appealing to him. The real me wouldn't have been.

"What's wrong, *mi amiga?*" he asked. Then he reached out to touch my cheek. He was studying me steadily, like he really wanted to know me.

I shrugged and looked away. I didn't want to share my thoughts right now, and besides, with him touching me, I felt too breathless to talk.

"*Deme un beso?*" He leaned closer and touched my chin with his finger, making me meet his gaze again.

I shrugged a little, like I didn't understand what he'd said.

I did, though. He wanted me to kiss him.

Chapter Fourteen

"What's the matter?" Hector asked. His voice was all low and husky. "Never been kissed?"

He was kind of joking, and I smiled while my stomach did cartwheels. "Sure," I said. "If you count Jonathon Jones pinning me against the jungle gym in fourth grade."

The truth was, I'd been kissed a couple of other times too, but he didn't need to know it. Those kisses hadn't made my heart pound the way it was right now.

"Jungle gym kisses don't count," he said, a smile crossing his handsome face.

He pulled me to him with infinite gentleness and pressed his lips to mine. His mouth was firm, confident, taking charge so I could just relax and follow his lead.

I tasted sweetness, like he'd just been drinking sugared coffee.

He whispered something I couldn't make out. I

breathed in the slightest hint of aftershave and reached up to touch his cheek, a little rough where he shaved.

He kissed me again, deeper this time. It felt warm and sweet and wonderful. And then it felt more strong than sweet, and I wanted to press my whole body hard into his. That feeling went on until I had to pull away to breathe.

"Wow," I whispered when I could.

"I know." His arm was still around me loosely, his hand stroking my hair. "I want to do more of that. Sometime when Mami and Tia Julia aren't right around the corner."

I did too. But I had to wonder whether Hector would be so interested in me if he knew who I really was.

Why was it that on the one weekend I felt like being alone to think things through, everything started happening?

I was basically staying in my room, working like a fiend on my IIFD scholarship application and my dress. I'd decided to go with a version of the dress I'd made for the party. I hadn't even pinned it up on the dress form at school, since I had the taffeta one as a model. It was coming along, but I kept finding little ways to improve it.

The application was a challenge too. For one thing, I had to decide what to say about my Spanish class. The committee would see my transcript, which would, best case, have a mediocre grade. So I couldn't get away with claiming fluency.

I skipped that section, filled out some easy stuff, and then came to the autobiography. "Why I Want to Study at IIFD," in one page. Yeah, right.

The phone was a welcome interruption.

"You've got to come out for coffee," Katie said. "I need to talk to you."

I said I couldn't, that I was working on my IIFD stuff. "Besides, I'm all freaked out about Hector," I confided. "Our project session got a little . . . hot."

"I knew it, Alicia," she said. "I knew he liked you. This is so great! He's a doll!"

"Yeah, but . . ." I trailed off, thinking about the whole complicated issue of my background and how Hector would feel about me if he knew. "It's not that simple. I thought if he liked me, things would be perfect, but I'm more confused than ever."

"I know what you mean. I feel the same way."

"You do?"

"Yes, because guess what!" Her voice was shrill with excitement.

"What?"

"Ralphie asked me out!"

"You're kidding! That's great! What are you guys doing?"

"Just going to the library to study for a history test. But as you well know, study sessions can turn into much, much more!"

She sounded so hopeful. While we squealed about it and planned what she should wear, I vowed inside that I would shoot Ralphie if he was just using her to pass a class.

"You sure you can't come out for coffee?" she asked wistfully.

"I wish I could, but I've got to get this stuff done. You know what it means to me."

"Yeah, it means you're leaving us," she said. "I don't want you to move away. You're a good friend."

"You'll be fine," I said around the lump in my throat. "You have Ralphie! I have to go."

I hung up the phone and looked down at my desk. There was the "Autobiographical Essay" page staring me in the face.

Why I want to go to IIFD: Because I don't belong anywhere else? Because I need a career before the system boots me out at eighteen? Because designing and drawing and sewing are the only things that hold me together sometimes?

I got on the computer and started drafting something, anything, figuring I could revise it later.

By the time I finished, I had way more than would fit in the one-page space on the application, and tears were rolling down my face.

It was just as well that an instant message popped up on my screen to distract me. It was Jimmy, wanting to know what I was doing.

"I'm busy on IIFD," I typed, and then grabbed for a tissue to blow my nose.

"Tough darts. I'm coming over," he said, and was off-line before I could beg him to stay away.

Oh, well. Jimmy was good for cheering a girl up. He only lived a couple of blocks away too, so by the time I'd washed my face and fixed my ratty hair, he was there. In fact, since Betsy and Ray tended to leave the doors unlocked when they were home, he let himself in and bounced up the stairs to my room.

"You will *not* believe this," he announced dramatically as he closed the door. "I got a phone call today, and let me just tell you, Katie's gonna hate paying me that gift certificate to Smithmore's."

"What?" I couldn't believe it.

My bedroom door flew open, hitting the dresser with a loud bang. Ray filled the doorway. "Alicia, you know the rules about boys in your bedroom," he boomed out.

I looked at Jimmy and giggled. "He's not . . ." I broke off.

"I'm telling her about my new boyfriend," Jimmy said. "I promise, I'll keep my hands to myself."

Ray crossed his arms over his chest and studied Jimmy, his eyes narrow.

"He means it, Dad," I said. I'd only recently started calling him that. "Jimmy is just a friend."

Ray's head cocked to one side as he studied me. "Well, all right." He turned to leave. "But the door stays open."

"Oh, Dad." But I had to grin at his departing back. It was kind of nice to have a protective male in my life.

"So did you hear what I said? I'm going out with Ralphie!" Jimmy sat on my floor, obsessively picking up scraps and threads from my sewing project and stacking them in a neat pile.

"To do what?" I asked.

"Studying," he said. "Geometry. But I'm taking him out for pizza afterwards."

"But do you know if he's . . . you know?"

"He's confused, and I'm going to unconfuse him," Jimmy said with supreme confidence.

I rolled my eyes and wondered what to do. Should I tell Jimmy that Katie already had a study date with Ralphie? Should I tell Katie about Jimmy? Or should I confront the two-timing twerp myself?

"I have to go. I'm gonna dye my spikes blond." Jimmy stood up. "Your dress is hot, Alicia. It's a lot cuter than Brianna's. You have a good chance for the scholarship."

"Thanks." I watched him trot toward the stairs and then turned back to my computer. But I wasn't in the mood to revise my emotional essay. I tried to IM Katie, but she wasn't online, and I was half glad; I didn't know whether to tell her about Jimmy's date with Ralphie or not.

Something made me type in the Altlives address, and immediately the screen went to a dark adobe-type church. It looked like there was some kind of festival going on: people were doing a sort of parade to the altar. Weirdly enough, some were crawling on their knees and a lot were barefoot.

And there was my birth family. They were barefoot, but otherwise in what must be their Sunday-best clothes, though the outfits looked pretty shabby to me. I noticed that the younger girl's dress was white with lots of embroidery on it, embroidery of the same style I liked to do.

As they slowly walked up to the front of the church, regret turned my stomach. I'd never considered before that when I lost my family, I lost my religion too. I mean, I'd grown up going to church with my foster family, and I believed in God. But apparently, judging from the candles and pictures and crucifixes around the church, I was supposed to have been a Catholic.

When the group got to the altar, a priest blessed the older boy with the taped-together glasses. Then the mother lit a candle.

Next, the younger boy came forward, and then the little girl. Same process. I noticed that the father was putting some cash into the box beside the candles.

What was he thinking? They didn't have enough money for food! They shouldn't spend what little they had on some hokey ceremony.

The mother murmured something to the father, and he shepherded the kids away, holding the handicapped boy's arm to guide him through the darkened church.

The mother lit another candle. She said something to the priest, and he patted her shoulder and made the sign of the cross in the air.

My mother prayed for a moment, then lifted her face to look at the statue of Mary.

Tears ran down her face.

All of a sudden I knew exactly what was going on.

She'd lit a candle for me. She was thinking about me, and crying for me.

I put my head down on my desk and cried for a long time. I didn't know whether I wanted to hold on to the image of my mother's traumatized face, or excise it from my consciousness.

Sure, she was upset. Very upset.

But she had her whole family around to comfort her. She had her culture, her religion, her language.

Here I was, stuck all alone in a tiny little town outside of Pittsburgh, Pennsylvania. With nothing.

But even while I thought my usual resentful thoughts, there was a tiny thrill inside me.

My mother might have given me away, but she remembered me. She still thought about me. She still missed me.

And maybe someday I could find her again!

A little tapping sound distracted me from my thoughts. I glanced up at the computer screen and saw that my family was getting into a horribly beat up car.

Tap-tap-splat.

The sound was coming from my window. I walked over. When had it gotten dark? What time was it? Were Betsy and Ray already asleep?

Tap-tap-splat.

It sounded like a bunch of little stones hitting the window. I peered out, but couldn't see anything, so I opened it and leaned out.

"Alicia! I've got to see you. Can I come up?"

It was Hector.

Chapter Fifteen

I let him in. What else could I do?

By now it was dark. Betsy and Ray had gone to bed, and the house was quiet. So I closed the back door behind him as quietly as I could. Then I beckoned him into the kitchen.

"What's going on?" I asked.

Now that he was inside, he looked a little awkward. "I, um, was doing some Internet research and found some great stuff about migrants," he said. He gestured toward my laptop, and for the first time I realized I had it clutched against my chest. "You too?"

"No, I was just doing some other stuff." No way was I sharing that I'd been watching my birth family on some magic computer game!

"The truth is," he said, "I really wanted to see you again." He reached out and touched my hair, then ran his hand very slowly down the length of it.

The tender way he did it filled some kind of longing in my heart. Warmth spread through my chest as I looked up at him, unable to speak.

His mouth twisted into a smile. "You're so pretty. But it's not just that, Alicia. You really care about people." He put his hands on my shoulders and looked right into my eyes. "Your family, Isabella, migrants, your friends . . . there's so much love in you. I just . . . I really like that."

All the breath seemed to whoosh out of me. I loosened my grip on the computer and put it down on the kitchen table.

Hector cupped my face in his hands and bent toward me.

But just before our lips would have met, I heard something upstairs. I pulled away, motioned for Hector to be quiet, and tiptoed to the hallway.

"Is everything okay down there, Alicia?" It was Betsy's sleepy, worried voice. She came a couple of steps down, in her knee-length nightgown, her hair rumpled. "I thought I heard something."

Man, she'd developed Mom Radar fast. "I'm fine," I said. "I'm working on my scholarship application, and I got hungry. I'm just fixing a snack."

"Okay, well, don't stay up too late," she said.

"I won't."

I waited until I heard their bedroom door click shut. Then I turned back to the kitchen. "We've got to be quiet. I'm sure it's against the rules to have you here."

"Do you want me to leave?"

Was he kidding? I wanted him to stay and stroke my hair for, like, six hours. I grinned and shook my head. "No. Just be quiet."

He took me seriously, lowering his voice and putting his hand over mine. "Show me what you were finding online, and then I'll show you my stuff."

I opened my laptop and unlocked it. I didn't think the wireless Internet connection would have stayed live on the game, but there it was.

I tried to turn the computer away from him, but he'd caught a glimpse of somebody working in a field and looked intrigued. "What is it? It looks like a great site!"

I shook my head. "It's nothing," I said, and then felt like I was putting a curse on my birth family. They weren't nothing. Even if they were poor and *had* nothing, even if society didn't value them, they were people.

"Let me see." Hector pulled the computer away from me and opened it up. "Hey, that girl looks like you!"

"It's not me." I slipped beneath his arm to look closer—and to *be* closer to him, I admit it—and checked out what was happening on-screen.

There was my mother, bending to pick some sort of low-to-the-ground fruit or vegetable. Her hands moved as quickly as machines over the green plants.

Next to her was a teenage girl, about my age, picking much more slowly. Her head was down, her shoulders slumped.

A man came by and stopped where my mother was working. He said something to her that must have been harsh, judging from the stricken look on her face. She nodded and nudged the teen, and the man said something else and went on.

The teen looked up toward the departing man with an expression of pure hatred on her face.

"Hey, that *is* you!" Hector said.

I studied the girl's face. Despite the bad hair and bad clothes and bad teeth, he was right. I'd seen her in the mirror a thousand times. I'd even seen that defiant expression on my own face.

A creepy feeling spread over me. "I don't know," I said slowly. "It's this site that, like, lets me see my birth family, you know?" Even as I said it, I knew I sounded totally insane.

Hector looked skeptical. "That doesn't make sense. How could you find your birth family online? And get some kind of camera on their lives?"

"I don't know." I shook my head. "It doesn't make logical sense, but my social worker told me about the site. And that one girl at school, Rose Graham, she knows about it too."

"But if it's your birth family," Hector said, nodding toward the screen, "then why are you in the picture?"

"I don't know," I admitted.

"It's not even really you. It's some weird, not so pretty version of you."

Even though I completely agreed, I resented what he said. Because I was starting to suspect that what we were watching on-screen was some alternate version of my life. Like, the migrant version.

Naturally, Hector didn't like the way I looked in *that* life.

The mean guy had come back into the picture and was yelling at me and my mom. I saw myself yell back and wanted to shout a warning to that girl on the screen. I could tell that antagonizing the boss was not going to have a good outcome.

But my on-screen self continued to yell.

The boss made a threatening move toward me, and my birth mom stepped protectively in front of me.

The next thing I knew, the man I knew was my father limped up. He shook his fist at the boss and shouted something.

Now the two men started arguing. It looked like the fight could go either way: verbal or physical.

"I wish I knew what they were saying!" I moaned.

"Is there any way you can find out?" Hector sounded like he was pretty caught up in the action too.

I ran the cursor around the screen. "There was some way to switch to audio. I tried it once, but I couldn't understand them."

"Why not?"

"Because they were speaking Spanish!" I looked at him, and light dawned. "Let me try to find it."

Thirty seconds later, I clicked on a drop-down menu and the screen went black. An incomprehensible stream of Spanish rolled out.

"What are they saying?"

Hector held up a hand. "I think . . . he's firing the whole family."

"Because of me?"

"Sssh!" He started shaking his head. "Oh, man, that is so unfair."

"What?"

"You might as well switch back to video," he said,

sounding disgusted. "Not only did he fire them, they have to move out of their house right away. He's not even giving them one more night to pack."

I clicked keys until the video came back up. There we were—Mom, Dad, and me—trudging off the field while other workers stayed hunched low, picking vegetables.

I felt like crying. But I was also confused. "I can't figure out whether this is real or not," I said. "I mean, it feels real. It seems real. It's not like that documentary or something. But . . . I'm there. And I'm here too."

"It's like an alternate universe," Hector said. "Man, don't you want to find them? Do you think you could?"

All of a sudden, a little text box popped up to the screen. "ALTLIFE!" it said. "Do you choose to switch over?"

There was also a digital clock . . . counting down from five minutes.

"What does it mean?" Hector asked. "Do you know?"

"I think . . . it must be what you said," I said slowly. "It's an alternate universe. Where I never got abandoned. Where they kept me."

"This can't be true," Hector said. But he was watching with the same fascination I felt while the family trudged to their crappy-looking trailer and went inside.

Tears rolled down the mother's face. She said something to the teenage girl—me—and I went across the road to where the two younger kids were playing.

They all waved to an ancient-looking woman who'd apparently been watching them from her lawn chair, and went back to my family's trailer.

My mother stood before a picture with a candle in front of it. There was an urn and a little vase of flowers there too. It must be Jesus, some sort of shrine. A Catholic thing.

"Who's in the picture?" Hector asked, and as the camera zoomed in a little, I realized that it wasn't Jesus at all.

It was the older brother, the deaf one, as a much younger boy than when I'd seen him on Altlives before.

The mother started packing the candle, vase, and photo into a box, carefully wrapping everything in newspaper. The rest of the family kept glancing over at her, but no one approached.

"Who's that?" Hector repeated.

"Um, my older brother, I think."

"When did he die?"

"He's not dead!" I shook my head. "I don't know where he is on-screen, but he's alive. I've seen him before."

"Don't you know what the urn is for?" Hector asked. "That's a cremation urn. His ashes are in there."

I froze. "How is he dead? He was alive before."

"Looks like he died when he was a little kid."

"But the only thing that's different is that I'm there. . . ." I trailed off.

How could it be? My presence in the family seemed

like a curse. Somehow, keeping me meant that my older brother had died.

Why? How? "Did they just not have enough food for both of us, or what?"

"Don't cry." Hector pulled me to him.

"I'm not crying!" I pushed away, flicking wetness from my cheeks. "I'm mad. How can this be happening? I find my birth family, I have a chance to get back with them and not be all abandoned and everything, I even *like* my family. But if I'm with them, my brother dies and my family lose their jobs!"

"It's not fair," Hector agreed. "But you have to click 'no.' Your time is running out."

"Just 'no'? 'No' to my family, my real family?"

"If you switch," Hector said, "then you're almost not you anymore. You wouldn't have had your foster mom. You wouldn't have moved to Linden Falls."

He didn't say it, but I saw what he was thinking.

"I wouldn't have you, either."

"Right, not that I'm worth basing your decision on or anything, but . . . Betsy and Ray? Katie and Jimmy? The chance to go to design school?"

"You know about that?"

He nodded. "Brianna told me."

I let my breath out in a huge sigh. "I know I have to click 'no,' but I just can't reject my birth family like that."

Hector looked at the screen. "Hey, they're driving," he said. "Wonder where they'll go?"

I looked, and an idea took shape in my mind.

"Maybe I can say no to the switch," I said, "but yes to finding them."

"There's a highway sign," Hector said, squinting. "It says, 'Toralupe, 10 km.' "

"Where's that?"

He shrugged. "Look, you're running out of time."

The on-screen clock was down to fifteen seconds. "You do it, I can't," I said, hiding my face in his chest.

I felt him reach over my head and click something. That little sound felt like sharp scissors snipping the thin, fragile thread that had tied me to my birth family.

I let my tears flow.

Hector was great. He held me and let me cry out my pain and loss and loneliness, and when I started to come back to my right mind, I felt his strong arms around me, his hands patting my back. I heard his voice comforting me in soft Spanish . . . Spanish I could understand. Every single word.

"We will find them," he said in Spanish, over and over.

Finally I blew my nose. "How will we find them?"

"We can find out where that town is and go from there."

"You mean a road trip?" I wiped my eyes, then blew my nose again. "Just us two?"

He grinned. "That sounds pretty great."

"You pervert." But it did sound great, not that I thought for a minute we'd be allowed to do it.

Chapter Sixteen

Of course we weren't allowed to do a road trip. Issues like school, driver's licenses, and supervision got in the way.

But we did get help.

We told Betsy and Ray that we'd done Internet research to find my birth family, and gave them the locations we'd seen. It wasn't a complete lie, right? I mean, Altlives is at least a computer thing.

Ray went online and found some likely migrant camps, and then used his university connections to make contacts in the Southwest. At some point my social worker, Fred, got involved. He had to know we'd found my family through Altlives, but he didn't spill the beans to Betsy and Ray. Instead he helped locate records that confirmed what Ray was finding out. He also found some grant money that could help reunite birth families.

And now my family was coming to see us. Today.

The backyard was all decked out with balloons and crepe paper and a sign that said, BIENVENIDOS, JIMINEZ FA-

MILIA! Yep, Jiminez was my real, birth-family name. That had helped Ray to find them. And all this time I'd suspected that it was just a made-up name.

Hector was here, and Mami, and Isabella, who helped relieve the tension. But not much. I was still incredibly nervous.

Finally, Ray's car pulled up. My heart started pounding really hard.

Then they all got out, the family I'd only seen on the computer screen: my mom, my dad, my older brother (I felt like he'd come back from the dead!), and the two younger kids.

My birth parents looked nervous and awkward standing in the street.

"Come on, come meet her," Ray urged, and everyone came slowly up the walk and around the side to the backyard.

I watched with emotions roiling in my chest. After all these years, my parents were here. The parents who'd abandoned me.

My parents, who looked bent and old and shabby, their faces lined from years of hard work in the sun.

Everyone else fell back as the two walked toward me.

My mother's tears flowed. She walked right up to me and reached up to take my face in her hands. She studied me like I was as precious as gold.

"*Alicia mia,*" she murmured over and over, clucking her tongue.

I don't know what I expected to feel, but "nothing" wasn't on the list. Yet that was what happened. I didn't love the woman in front of me. I didn't hate her either. For years I'd been angry in the abstract about her abandoning me, but now that I knew the specifics of her life, I didn't exactly feel angry.

The fact was, I just didn't know her. And that seemed a little sad.

My father said something in Spanish. He was standing next to my mother but a little off to one side, studying me with equal intensity.

"He says they have prayed for this moment," Hector supplied.

"You are beautiful," my father added in Spanish.

Before Hector could translate, I waved my hand. I'd understood that one just fine.

Hector whispered something to my father, whose eyes lit up. He started singing in a super-quiet voice.

"Papitas, papitas
Para mamá.
Las quemaditas,
Para papá."

The years fell away as I looked into his eyes. I was a little girl again, adored by my daddy and adoring him back.

He held out his arms, and before I could think, I was in them, clasped to his chest, tears running down my face.

He sang a few more lines and then choked up, and we just hugged. When I finally pulled away to look at him, his face was wet too.

"Alicia, you are all grown up," he said. He was

speaking Spanish, but simply, like you would talk to a little kid, with accompanying gestures.

Miraculously, I understood him.

There was a strange grunting noise beside me, and when I turned, there was my older brother. He was pointing at me and gesturing to his mother, and she signed back. He kept shaking his head and moving his arms like he was rocking a baby.

Obviously he didn't understand how the little sister he vaguely remembered could be a tall teenager.

I spotted Isabella. Unlike the adults, who were pretending to occupy themselves getting food and examining the azaleas, she stood staring at our reunion with a curious expression on her face.

I gestured her over and tapped my brother on the arm. I squatted down to her size so she could see. "He's my big brother," I explained, "but he hasn't seen me in a really long time, since I was your size." Slowly I stood up, pointed at myself, and pointed at him. *"Hermana,"* I said, moving my lips in an exaggerated way. *"Hermano."*

With so many Spanish speakers around, I would have normally been embarrassed by my bad pronunciation of the Spanish words for "sister" and "brother." But my brother was deaf—he couldn't hear accents, but I figured he could maybe read lips.

He cocked his head to one side and pointed at me. "Ah-ah-ah," he grunted.

His mother—*my* mother—nodded excitedly. "Alicia," she spelled with her fingers.

I realized I could follow her finger spelling because,

like a lot of little kids, I'd learned it in grade school. I tapped his arm. "I love you," I spelled out, but he only looked puzzled.

"What are you doing?" Isabella asked.

"I'm trying to tell him I love him, but I can't get him to understand." Then I realized I'd been spelling it in English. "Oh, duh. I need to spell it in Spanish."

"It's *te amo*," she said, "but you could also use this sign." She held out her hand with her pointer, pinkie, and thumb extended. "I saw it on *High Five*."

Little genius. Why couldn't I be as smart as Isabella?

I did it, and checked him for understanding. A broad smile crossed his face and he grabbed me in a bear hug. Too tight, but I didn't mind. I knew what no one else did, except maybe Hector: My living here instead of with my family had somehow saved my brother's life.

I hugged him back hard.

When we finally parted, someone tugged at my sleeve. I expected it to be Isabella, but it was one of the younger kids, the girl. My sister.

Anger swept through me. She'd been raised by my parents and I hadn't.

She pulled her brother, *my* little brother, forward. They both chanted out some clearly rote phrase of welcome.

"*Gracias,*" I said without a whole lot of thankfulness in my heart.

"You have a nice house." The little girl's English was heavily accented. She must be learning it in school, which meant she must get the chance to go to school, at least sometimes. "Nice clothes." She reached out toward my vest and fingered it, clearly envious.

Envious. Of *me*. How bizarre.

I'm sure everyone expected me to hug these kids, but I wasn't interested, and I was pretty sure they weren't either. We were all jealous of each other. We hadn't asked to be an instant family.

But as big sister, I figured I had to be the grown-up. I squatted down in front of them. "I hope I can get to know you. And I'm glad you speak English." It was the only honest thing I could say, but it was a start.

"Can we have some food?" the brother asked.

"Sure, go ahead. Eat all you want." I waved my hand toward the table, heaped high, and they ran toward it like they were starving.

Which made me realize that maybe they were. "You too," I gestured to my older brother. "Go eat. *Comes.*" I mimed eating with my hands.

He grinned and turned toward the table. My father followed him, obviously feeling a need to supervise.

Or maybe he was starving too.

That left me standing there with my mother, feeling awkward. I was very conscious that she wanted me to hug her as I'd hugged my father. But I couldn't do it.

Giving me away had to have been her decision. I couldn't imagine that my father would have made her do it. And even if there were reasons why they had to, reasons I was starting to understand, it still hurt.

She touched my arm. "You come live to us?" Her

English was terrible, but clearly she'd practiced saying that one phrase.

"You want me? *Tu me quieres?*"

"*Si, si, si.*" She nodded. "You come live to us."

"Wait." I looked around the yard: at Betsy and Ray, pretending not to watch us; at Mami, urging food on my skinny social worker; at Hector, talking with my father. I thought about Linden High, about Katie and Jimmy, about the IIFD announcement, which would come next week.

In a way, I wished I could go back, start over. But I knew I couldn't. This was me now, and this was where I had to stay.

I turned to my mother. "*Es mi casa,*" I said, gesturing toward the house. Then I waved my arm around the yard. "*Mi amigos.*"

She started to correct my bad Spanish, then registered what I was saying. Her eyes didn't tear up, but they got terribly, terribly sad.

"Come inside," I said, tugging at her arm. "I want to show you something."

As I pulled her toward the house, Betsy mouthed, "Are you okay?" to me.

I nodded and smiled at her. She looked so worried. As usual.

Betsy and Ray needed me to worry about.

Upstairs in my room, I pulled out my IIFD dress. "Look. For school." I showed it to Mami. Then I pulled out an IIFD brochure and showed it to her.

The brochure had several languages, including

Spanish, and I watched as she carefully worked her way through the paragraph that explained the scholarship. When she looked up at me, her eyes weren't sad anymore. "All go good," she said.

I turned away. I think she meant they'd done the right thing giving me away. Which really hurt! I mean, sure, I had the chance to go to a great school, but I'd missed out on a mother's love all those years.

I turned back to express my anger, and I saw tears running down her face. My hand went out, automatically, to wipe them away. "Why? *Por qué?*"

"*Mi corazón,*" she said. "My heart . . . how you say? Achy breaky."

I was crying too, but her words made me laugh a little. It made some sort of sense that her English came from country songs, but "Achy Breaky Heart"?

She walked over to my dresser and studied the photos I had there: my first foster mom, my foster brother and sister, Katie and Jimmy and me being crazy. She zeroed in on my first foster mom. "*Quién es?*"

"*Mi madre,*" I said simply. "She took care of me from when I was three." I held my hand low to the ground, the height of a toddler.

She shook her head, and her tears flowed more. "*Mi corazón,*" she said, patting her heart.

My own heart was melting toward her as I saw what giving me up had done to her. I'd get Hector to talk to them later about the specifics of why they'd given me up, but understanding, and really seeing, the intense pain of it made a huge difference to me.

At the same time, I was afraid we would both lose

ourselves in grief. So I turned to what always made me feel better. Designing. "You like my dress?" I asked her, holding it up again.

She grabbed a couple of tissues and wiped her face, then came over to study it. A smile came over her face. "You make?" she asked.

"Si."

She studied the seams and the hem and then held it up to me. She nodded her approval. *"Es perfecto,"* she said. *"Pero . . ."*

I knew a "but" when I heard one. "What?"

She touched the vest I wore, the one with all the embroidery. *"Mas bonito,"* she said.

Prettier. Of course, it was.

Shyly, she opened the buttons of the ragged black sweater she wore. Inside, the neckline of her cotton blouse was covered with wild, colorful embroidery.

The pattern of it was amazingly like my vest.

"You make?" I asked her.

She nodded.

We both looked from one to the other. And then, with big smiles, we finally hugged each other.

Chapter Seventeen

"Your attention, students, please!"

Mrs. Leaf stood at the front of the sewing lab, waving a piece of paper. But it was the end of the last day of class, and we were all too rowdy to listen.

Until some of the people up front heard her say, "IIFD."

"It's the scholarship!" The shrill announcement made its way around the room, and we all headed for our tables. My heart pounded with excitement, even though I kept trying to tell myself I wouldn't win.

Katie grabbed my hand. "I know you'll get it!"

"No way," I said, shaking my head as we reached our table and sank into our seats.

Still, some tiny part of me felt hopeful.

"We've just received word about the IIFD scholarship," Mrs. Leaf said. "And without further ado, I'd like to ask you to congratulate Brianna Davis, this year's scholarship winner!"

We all clapped. But even in the midst of my crushing disappointment, I noticed how uncelebratory the celebration was. And I remembered how Brianna had said that no one really liked her—they were just afraid of her.

Katie put an arm around me and Jimmy mimed crying, and I felt a little better.

As the clapping died away, I turned to Brianna and found her looking at me. To my surprise, she wasn't gloating. "You could have entered a different dress," she said.

Of course she was right. My design had been off-beat already. And at the last minute, in honor of my mother, I'd added outrageous ethnic embroidery to the neckline and sleeves.

"Yours was too wild," she continued. "You sabotaged yourself."

I could have made a mean remark about sabotage—after all, she'd messed with my dress form—but somehow I didn't have enough fight in me. "I gotta be me," I said instead. "And I'm glad you get to go."

She gave me the first nonsarcastic smile I'd ever seen on her. "You can't even believe how happy I am to get out of here."

Mrs. Leaf called out, "I'm not finished, class," and after a couple of minutes she got our attention again. "There's a postscript on the letter that makes honorable mention of Alicia Jiminez," she said. "While you didn't win an early-admission scholarship, Alicia, they encourage you to apply at the end of high school."

Katie and Jimmy led the cheering, and I basked in it. I didn't feel terribly disappointed. The truth was, I'd found a home and friends here at Linden High, and to uproot myself and go over to Madrid would have been really, really hard.

Not only that, but my birth family had plans to settle in the region too. Fred was helping them look into farm work and housing assistance, and they seemed ready to make a change.

So Linden Falls was home, at least for now.

The bell rang, and as I walked out into the crowded hallway, loud with last-day voices and banging lockers, I heard a familiar sound.

"Ah-ah-ah-ah-ah. Livin' la vida loca!"

Ralphie. I rolled my eyes. But I wasn't really bothered. Truth to tell, my life *was* crazy these days, but not in a bad way.

He came up behind us and covered Katie's eyes. "Guess who," he said.

She turned and giggled.

And then—get *this!*—he draped his arm around her and tugged her away from us.

Katie gave Jimmy an apologetic shrug and followed him.

I spun on Jimmy. "I thought you were dating him!"

"He was using me for my mind," Jimmy said with a dramatic sigh. "As soon as he found out he'd passed geometry, he dropped me."

"Are you upset?"

Jimmy shook his head. "He never did have enough class for me. Now, up ahead is someone pretty classy. . . ."

I looked in that direction and saw Hector waiting for me with a big smile on his face.

"He's mine," I warned Jimmy.

"I know. I have other fish to fry." He veered off toward where a new boy sat alone.

I walked toward Hector and was surprised when he pulled me into his arms. We'd been seeing each other, and sharing a little affection in private, but we'd kept it light at school. Neither of us wanted to rub it in to Brianna.

But she was nowhere in sight now, and anyway she would head for Madrid this summer. "What's this all about?" I asked his neck, snuggling in.

"I'm happy," he said. "I heard about the scholarship."

"You're happy I didn't win?" I asked, pulling away.

"I'm happy you got honorable mention," he said. "Now you'll have time for more Spanish tutoring."

Involuntarily, I grinned. Our tutoring sessions had consisted mostly of endearments lately. But I was doing okay in class now; I'd finished the year with a very respectable C after the success of our extra-credit project on migrants. The video of my birth parents had clinched it; ours was the only project in the show that made people cry.

"And most of all, I'm happy you get to stay. Your folks will be nearby too. No excuses to leave."

I leaned back in his arms. Hector looked handsome and possessive and determined to be my boyfriend.

And I had no objections at all.

Discover more
secret lives in
other books by
Lee McClain!

Turn the page
to get a taste of two
more Altlives novels...

MY ALTERNATE
LIFE

Chapter One

I didn't plan to jump out of a moving car. And I definitely didn't plan to land in a cow pie.

It's just that Fred wasn't listening when I said I really, really, really didn't want a new family.

Fred's streaky gray hair flowed down the back of his tie-dyed shirt, and his voice was classic social worker. "There's your new high school," he said. "It's small. Homey. You'll make friends fast."

But I saw the squat, light-brick building a different way. Small schools are cliquish and nosy, and there's not a lot of space for difference.

And I, Trinity B. Jones, am different.

Not to mention that I'm totally urban. So when I saw the field full of cows right next to the school, I lost it and jumped.

Fortunately, I was wearing my leather jacket and jeans, so I didn't get scraped up by the strands of barbed wire I flew through. And I'm not totally stupid—I grabbed Fred's cell beforehand. My plan was to call Nate, my boyfriend back in the city where

I so fully belonged, and get him to beg, borrow, or steal a car and come rescue me.

The cow pie gunked up my plans. "Euew!" I screamed and knelt there in the tall grass, trying to wipe off my jacket. It was the most expensive thing I owned. A gift from Nate.

Behind me I could hear Fred's old Ford screeching to a halt.

"Are you okay?" asked a girl's voice above me.

I looked up to see a line of girls dressed in workout clothes. They were leaning over the fence that separated the school from the cow pasture, squinting in the late-afternoon sun.

Fred came panting up behind me. "Trinity B. Jones," he said, "what do you think you're doing? You could have been killed, and just when—" He squatted down in the tall grass beside me. "Are you all right?"

"I'm fine," I said, "but my jacket isn't. They need to curb their cows around here."

"She landed in cow crap!" giggled one of the girls.

"Don't talk trash," said another girl.

I rolled my eyes. If that was trash talk, this place was even more backward than I'd thought.

"Trinity," Fred said, taking hold of my clean arm, "get back in the car. You know I'll have to write an incident report about this."

"And get me sent to Saint Helen's?" I asked. *That would be cool.* Saint Helen's Home for Girls was in the same neighborhood as my old foster family, which meant the same neighborhood as Nate.

"In your dreams," Fred said. "Come on, back in the car."

"Flag Team! Line up! Competition is one week away!" came a voice behind the line of girls.

I sighed and headed back toward the car, letting Fred fuss with a little scrape on my knuckle while I used his bandanna to wipe off my smelly jacket.

After we were inside, Fred started driving again, but he was at least taking me more seriously. "Trinity, listen to me. This family is perfect for you. What's more, Susan is interested in adopting you, if everything works out well."

"Yeah, right." I knew that would never happen, not at my age. I'd been to enough adoption picnics to know that adoptive parents wanted a cute little baby to hold, not a fifteen-year-old with brown skin, a 34-C, and a nose ring.

"I thought you liked Susan." Fred cut off the main road and turned right in between two fields. A pickup truck drove by and the driver gave us a little wave. Three fingers, toot-toot of his horn. Where I was from, that would have been a gang signal.

"Susan's fine," I said. "It's not that."

"She thinks you're more than fine," he said. "She's very impressed with your academic achievements and she thinks she has a lot to offer you. She's a lawyer, you know."

"Yeah, big deal." My regular social worker had already given me the lowdown on how Susan worked a lot in family court, and that was why she got interested in foster care. Susan had come into the city to meet me a couple of times. She was a real business-woman, all suits and sensible shoes, and she talked smart. Nice enough. But I didn't want to be her good deed for the year.

We were getting closer to the house; I could tell from how Fred turned onto another, even narrower road.

My heart started pounding harder. This was really going to happen and I didn't want it to. I just wanted Nate, so he could wrap his big arms around me and tell me everything would be okay.

But there was something else I wanted even more, and because I was pushed into a corner, I blurted it out. "I don't want a new family, I want my real mom."

Fred glanced over at me. "Trinity, that's not going to happen."

"Why not? If she knew the Holmsteads put us all out on the street, she'd take me." The Holmsteads had been my foster parents for five years. It was nothing great, but it wasn't bad.

Fred shook his head. "She couldn't take care of you. She would want nothing more than for us to find you a permanent adoptive family." He turned into a long dirt driveway.

We approached a big white house. The front porch had rocking chairs and a swing. A couple of big trees stood in the yard, and an old Volvo was parked beside the house.

Balloons bobbed on the front porch railing and a computer-generated banner read, "Welcome, Trinity!"

158

That made me feel funny. Sort of happy, in the babyish part of myself, because I'd never had birthday parties and all that, and when I was a kid, I'd really wanted to.

But it also seemed kind of fake. Susan didn't know me and she didn't know how it was all going to work out, so why act like everything's beautiful?

And the front door was opening, and there was Susan, plus a teenage girl about my age. Oh, yeah, her *real* daughter. She'd been too busy with all her social activities to meet me when Susan had.

They were both smiling and waving.

I felt like I might get sick. Everything was moving along faster than the race car video games Nate and I loved to play. But I was going in the wrong direction: away from what I wanted, and toward what I didn't want.

Fred stopped the car but, thankfully, he didn't open the door right away. He turned to look at me. "You okay, kiddo?" he asked.

I had to swallow a couple of times before I could answer. "No."

"Look," he said, reaching into his shirt pocket. "Before we go in, I have something for you. It might make you feel better about everything." He handed me an envelope.

"Thanks." I was surprised. He'd only taken over my case a month ago. And in a whole long string of social workers, not one had ever given me a gift. I hoped it was money. "Can I open it now?"

A funny smile crinkled his face, and a sparkle in his

159

eyes made him look like a mad little elf. "No, wait until later, when you're on the computer," he said.

By the time "later" came, my head was spinning. Maybe it was the cake Susan had made—super sweet, yellow with chocolate icing, my favorite. Someone must have told her.

It was nice of her to make it and I managed to choke some down, but I was uptight. For one thing, the daughter, Kelly, wasn't exactly my type. She was skinny and tailored and tense. But Susan clearly thought that, since we were both fifteen, we were going to be the best of friends.

"Now, you each have your own bedroom," Susan said, upstairs, after Fred had left and we'd brought in all my stuff. "You share the study and bathroom."

My bedroom looked like the set of *City Girls Go Country:* hardwood floors, fringy little rugs, and ruffled curtains tied back with yellow ribbons.

I could tell Susan had decorated it and wanted me to gush. Well, tough. Sure, I was grateful to have my own room. But this place totally wasn't me.

I was chrome and black leather, not flowers and country charm. Just more evidence that this wasn't the right place for me.

When I saw the computer in the study, I brightened up. While I was here, until I came up with a new plan, at least I could stay in touch with my old friends. "I need to check my e-mail," I said.

"I need the computer tonight too," Kelly said quickly. "Homework."

"I'm sure you two can negotiate that," Susan said. "Kelly, you've got laundry in the basement to fold and put away, and Trinity, you need to get your things organized for school tomorrow."

"Whoa," I said. "Wait up. I can't start school tomorrow."

"Why not?" Susan's eyebrows went up just a little.

Because I'm freaking out here. "I, um, I'm not registered. Don't I have to do some official stuff first?"

"I've got it all taken care of," Susan said. "I'll go in with you tomorrow and we'll finalize your classes, but that's it. You should be able to start with your homeroom period and go through the day."

"Mom's efficient," Kelly said.

I excused myself, went into the bright pink bathroom I was to share with Kelly, and threw up.

When I came back out and went into my bedroom, Susan was waiting. "Are you okay?" she asked.

I nodded. "I just haven't been feeling all that great. Maybe I have a little flu. Maybe I shouldn't go to school tomorrow."

Susan patted the bed beside her and I sat down, keeping a good foot of distance between us. I could tell she wanted to put her arm around me, but no matter what her title was, she wasn't my mother. And I wasn't staying. So there was no point in getting all lovey-dovey.

"Trinity," she said, "I know this must be very difficult for you, leaving your old home and starting out new."

"It's okay," I lied.

Obviously, she didn't believe me. "Even though it's

hard, I want you to go to school tomorrow unless you're really sick. We believe in good school attendance in this family."

I stared down at my knees. I wasn't really sick, but I dreaded the thought of starting out new, in the middle of tenth grade, at some school where everyone already had their friends.

"Kelly will help you get through the day," she said, "and we'll make sure you know your way around. It's a small school, so I think you'll find it a lot friendlier than what you're used to."

"Sure." I could tell there was no use arguing with Susan. After all, she was a lawyer.

Anyway, it was only for a few days, just long enough for me to come up with a plan. I could stand anything for a few days.

"Good girl." She scooted over and gave me a little squeeze around the shoulders.

I went into my fence-post act. No way was I hugging her back.

She stood up. "Now, I'll bet you can get on that computer before Kelly comes back up."

The thought of e-mailing Nate made me smile. "Thanks," I said, and meant it.

Moments later I was online, and just as I'd hoped, there was an e-mail from Nate.

Hey, babe, I miss you, want you, love you. Scope the scene and tell me when, I'll snag a car and come visit. It's not the same around here without you.

I wrapped my arms around my middle as I read it again and again. Nate wasn't much of a talker but he was sincere and he had respect. We'd been together for a year and before I left, we swore we'd stay faithful to each other.

I answered e-mails from some other friends and surfed a little. Kelly wasn't back and I figured she was talking to her mom. I didn't feel tired, more like highstrung and worried, and I didn't know what to do with myself. Then I remembered the card old Fred had given me. I got it out and opened it.

The card itself looked like Fred, with a swirled design and a cosmic poem inside. No money, unfortunately.

Fred's message said, "If you ever feel like going home, check out this site." And there was a Web address.

Oh, geez. Probably some psychological site for unhappy teens. But what the hey, I qualified for that! I typed in the address: *www.ALTLIVES.com.*

What came up was a game. Some gift! I mean, I know social workers don't make much money, but to tell me he's giving me a gift and then point me to a Web site with some silly computer game . . . oh, well. Fred wasn't the first social worker to disappoint me.

Just for fun, I started playing.

The first prompt was *A car shows up in your driveway. Fred's driving.*

You:

I'd played a few old-fashioned games like this before: a lot of text, kind of boring. But because the name was Fred, I wondered if old Fred was involved in making up this game. So I played along. What would I do if Fred showed up in my driveway?

GET IN, I typed.

Fred starts driving. Where do you want to go?

You: TELL HIM I WANT TO GO BACK TO THE CITY.

Fred drives.

There was some la-di-da stuff about driving past cows and horses, just like when Fred and I had come out here, which was weird. But I answered all the questions.

Once we got to the city, the game asked me where I wanted to go. I thought about it.

Did I really want to go back to the Holmsteads? After they'd gotten sick of fostering teenagers and kicked us all out?

And anyway it was just a game. I figured that once I got as specific as a single address, it wouldn't work anymore.

But what the heck. I was getting bored with the game. I typed in Nate's address.

Are you sure? the computer asked.

I blinked.

YES, I'M SURE.

As you approach Nate's house, you see him coming out. What do you do?

HUG HIM! I typed.

You're still in the car.

Oh, duh. I typed, GET OUT OF THE CAR.

He doesn't see you because he's talking to some-one.

WHO IS HE TALKING TO?

Jessica and Tanika.

I stared at the screen as my stomach knotted up. This was truly bizarre. I knew Jessica and Tanika. They were twins. And they'd been hot for Nate as long as I could remember.

I DON'T BELIEVE YOU.

For, like, ten seconds, a visual flashed on the screen. Sure enough, it was the front of Nate's house. Jessica and Tanika each had one of his hands, and they were pulling him down his front porch steps as he laughed and tried to resist, but not very hard.

MY ABNORMAL
LIFE

Chapter One

Okay, so it was a dumb idea, convincing my retarded sister Danielle to hide in the back of an Ethan Allen furniture truck.

But as I hunched on the bottom porch step of a strange house in a strange town on a damp January day, it was the best escape plan I could manage.

Nothing had gone right since Social Services had stuck their collective noses into our lives one week ago. This was the worst yet. I was waiting outside because I couldn't stand to watch Dani get settled in her new home.

Without me.

That was when I saw the truck and heard the furniture movers complaining that their next stop was all the way in the middle of Pittsburgh.

Where Dani, Mom, and I lived. Hmmmm.

The seed of my big idea planted itself in my mind, and I stood up and strolled closer to the truck, keeping my eyes down, making myself as invisible as I could.

Behind me, the door to Dani's new home burst open and a guy my age slammed out onto the front porch. "Don't pay any attention to what I want," he yelled. "You never do!"

The door closed behind him.

Even I, Miss Zero Experience, could see that the boy was sexy. He had broad, powerful shoulders and dark brown hair that curled over the sheepskin collar of his coat.

And, oh my gosh, his eyes. I mean, I have brown eyes, but like everything else about me, they're ordinary and forgettable.

This boy's brown eyes looked like melted chocolate. They drooped down at the outside corners, like he was just a little bit sleepy. But there was nothing sleepy about the athletic way he took the porch steps in one leap and strode down the walk.

I hadn't been this close to a good-looking boy in forever. Mostly I'd just watched them out our apartment window, or on TV. So I got a disloyal flash of, "Hey, maybe it won't be so bad in this town," as I watched him walk toward me.

My prince, coming to my rescue?

"Why can't you people solve your own problems?" he yelled in my direction.

My warm, fuzzy feeling evaporated. "Us people? Excuse me?" I marched toward him, ready to fight. I may be short but I'm strong.

His cell phone rang and he turned away like I wasn't even there. "Yeah?" he said into it. "Oh, just another Little Orphan Annie my folks have taken in. I was supposed to be home to, quote, make her feel welcome, but I'm bailin'."

"We're not orphans," I protested to his broad back.

Just at that moment, Dani came out onto the porch. She was crying with her mouth wide open, loud wails that reached into my chest and pierced my heart.

I ran up the steps and wrapped my arms around her. "Hey, it's okay," I said, even though it wasn't. I stroked her tangled, light brown hair and patted her bony back.

Her wails slowed, then stopped. "I not stay here," she said, her voice shaky. "I stay *you*."

My point exactly. I looked up at the screen door of the house, where our social worker Fred and the new foster mom stood watching.

"You can visit each other," Fred said.

"After she has a few days to settle in." The foster mom crossed her arms over her chest. Her chin was pointy like a witch's. "Rose, she needs to hear from you that it's okay for her to stay here."

"You want me to lie?" I said it quietly so that Dani, whose head was now buried in my shoulder, wouldn't hear.

The foster mom's lips tightened. "Say your good-byes," she said. "Fred, we need to nail down some details."

The two of them disappeared back into the house.

Dani clung to me. "I stay *you*," she repeated over and over.

Her words tore at my heart, and what made it

worse was that it was all my fault. If I hadn't tried to shoplift food from a new store whose owner I didn't know, the police would never have found out how Dani, Mom, and I were living.

Stupid, stupid, stupid.

It was bad enough being taken away from Mom, not to mention my apartment and my neighborhood and everything I knew. But I'd thought Dani and I could stay together. Putting us in separate homes in the same small town was the bright idea of our counselors at St. Helen's Home for Girls.

After having known us for all of one week, they'd decided I was overly responsible and prematurely adult. And they thought Dani, at eight, was too attached to me.

Well, duh. What choice did we have?

And what was so bad about being responsible and attached?

So now, just because I'd answered some questions wrong in their interviews, I couldn't stay with Dani and help her get used to a new place.

My grandma's words came back to me: "You're this baby's guardian angel," she'd said when Dani was born with Down syndrome. "With the good Lord's help, you have to keep her safe, whatever your mother and father do."

Well, Gram, I thought, looking up toward heaven, *you better tell the good Lord to step in quick.*

Dani wrapped herself around me like a monkey and I carried her down the porch stairs.

And there sat the truck, wide open. The back of it

was half full of furniture. The delivery guys were inside the next-door neighbors' house.

"Hey, Dani," I said, "want to play a game?"

She lifted her head. "What game?"

I dug a used tissue out of my jeans pocket and wiped her nose. "See that truck?" I said. "We're gonna play hide-and-seek in it. Hold on."

I glanced back at the doorway of Dani's new foster home. Still empty. Then I scrambled up the ramp that led into the back of the truck and looked around. There were a couple of big dressers we could hide behind and some green padded blankets to pull over the top of us. Perfect!

"Hey," said a voice outside the truck.

I froze.

"Are you crazy? What're you doing?"

Slowly, I turned around.

It was Mr. Sexy. "I gotta go," he said into his cell phone, and stuffed it in the pocket of his windbreaker. "Get outta there," he said to me. "Any minute now, they're going to shut this truck and drive off. You can't play in there."

I put Dani down but kept my hands on her shoulders to soothe her. "We're not playing," I said.

He came closer, hoisting himself up to sit on the back of the truck. "My mom's gonna kill you."

"Look, just get out of here before somebody sees you," I hissed. "We're taking care of our own problems, okay? We're trying to go back home."

"You're stowing away?" He sounded the slightest bit impressed.

Lee McClain

"It dark in here," Dani said.

"I know. We're playing cave." It was a game we played whenever the lights got turned off at home.

Dani started to cry. "I no like cave!"

I sighed. "Look," I said, kneeling down to face her. "We're going to go for a ride in this truck. A long ride, but I'll be right here with you all the time. And when it opens up again, we'll be back home."

"Are you out of your mind?" asked the boy.

"Just get out of here so nobody sees you," I snapped. "This isn't your business."

"Brian!" a woman's voice called. "Did you see where Dani and her sister went?"

I heard more people coming this way. "Off the truck, kid," said a male voice. "We're heading out."

I put my hands together to pantomime a prayer to the kid. And then I had to focus on Dani. "Come on, down here," I whispered, and pulled her behind the biggest dresser with me. "Look, we'll put this blanket over us. Be real quiet!"

A big sliding door came down, blocking all the light from the back of the truck.

The engine rumbled to life.

Dani started crying again.

As the truck started moving, I hugged her tightly and tried to feel good about getting away. I'd always taken care of our family. Usually, though, I had a little more time to sort through alternatives and make a plan. This time I'd made a snap decision.

Sometimes being responsible sucks. Because what if you make a really big mistake?

174

At least we're together. I hugged Dani tighter. *And we're away from that mean foster mom*.

The truck screeched to a halt. Angry voices argued outside.

"What that man talk about?" Dani asked me.

"Sssh." I put my hand over her mouth, but gently so she wouldn't get mad. "We're playing a game, remember? We have to be really quiet."

"I no like cave!" she said, still crying a little.

The back of the truck opened with a screechy metal-on-metal sound, and light flooded in.

"Anybody back here?" a man's voice called.

"Well, they're hardly likely to answer you," came the foster mom's witchy voice.

Dani jumped out of my grip. "Here we are!" she crowed.

Caught!

I let my head sink down into my hands for one tiny moment. Then, slowly, I stood up and walked out into view.

Dani danced around, all happy, thinking the game was over and she'd won. The foster mom lit into the furniture guys for not checking their truck.

Fred, the social worker, glared at me. "What were you thinking?" he asked. "You could have gotten hurt or lost. And it's not just you, it's your sister in question."

I clamped my mouth shut and looked away. We would've been fine. I knew my way around my home turf and I'd been taking care of Dani for years.

But no way would a social worker believe in me. That wasn't in his job description.

My eyes landed on the foster brother, Mr. Sexy. "You told," I accused him. "You ran to Mommy and told."

He lifted his hands. "It wasn't me. I was ready to let you go."

"Yeah, right."

He nodded toward Fred. "It was that guy. He's weird. It's like he could see you through the truck. He knew right away where you went."

"Maybe he just has a lot of experience with deceitful young people," said the foster mom. Apparently she'd finished with the furniture guys and was ready to turn her scolding tongue on us.

"Come on out, girls," Fred said, and Dani, little traitor that she was, ran to him. He helped her off the back of the truck.

I got down on my own—nobody was rushing to give *me* a hand—and right away the foster mom got on my case. "You endangered your sister. I had my reservations about you before, considering the shape she's in, but now I'm certain you're a bad influence."

That remark on top of everything else stunned me. All I'd done for eight years was take care of Dani. And now this stranger had the nerve to tell me I'd done a bad job?

Tears pushed at the back of my eyes and my throat started hurting.

Mr. Sexy must have noticed. "Mom, lighten up," he said.

She spun around. "You're just as bad, Brian," she snapped. "You saw them get into that truck and didn't tell me. If anything had happened, it would have been your fault. And with all your gifts, you should know better."

Brian's head dropped and he turned around. "I don't want 'em here anyway," he muttered as he walked away.

Through my misery I wondered about his so-called gifts. What were they? Or was being born normal in a houseful of retarded kids considered a gift in itself?

"Come on," Fred said to me. "We're late. We have to get you settled in your new home, and I know your foster parents are eager to meet you."

I dreaded the thought.

"Dani, let's go get a snack," said the foster mom.

My little sister loved food. She turned and followed the woman toward the house.

" 'Bye, Dani," I called with a little crack in my voice. "See you soon."

"No contact for two weeks," said the foster mom over her shoulder, looking at Fred. "And only phone calls and supervised visits for the first couple of months. If you can arrange that, I won't report this little incident to the agency."

Two weeks? First couple of months? But there was so much I hadn't told The Witch about Dani. How to get her to take a bath. How *Sesame Street* always calmed her down. How she liked to be sung to sleep.

My chest felt empty, like someone had pulled my heart out of it. I took a step toward Dani.

Fred put his arm around me and guided me toward his old beater of a car. "It'll be good for you girls to settle into your own homes," he said. "I know the McGraws want to get you involved in some school activities."

School activities? That was the last thing I wanted to think about.

"Great," I said, not bothering to hide my sarcasm. I was too busy trying to hide my tears.

MY ABNORMAL *LIFE*

LEE McCLAIN

"But I'm not normal!"

Fifteen-year-old Rose Graham has never been to school. She's never had a date. She certainly never knew she was gorgeous. She's been too busy shoplifting food, keeping Social Services off her family's case, and taking care of her little sister.

Now, plunged into a foster family in affluent Linden Falls, she's supposed to act normal. But everything seems so trivial when all Rose wants is to get her family back together. At least she has the Altlives computer game to help her cope. And Brian Johnson's broad shoulders to drive her crazy....

KATIE
MAXWELL
CIRCUS OF THE DARNED

I've given up all hope of having a normal life. As if things aren't freaky enough traveling around Europe with a group of witches, mediums, and magicians who make up the GothFaire, now I also have to cope with a mysterious man who wants to steal my horse!

I just want to go on a date with Benedikt, but when your boyfriend's a vampire, nothing is easy. Not only is Ben keeping secrets from me, but somehow, I raised an entire battlefield of warring Viking ghosts—all of whom refuse to be sent back.

And I thought all I had to worry about was what to wear on my date...

Didn't want this book to end?

There's more waiting at **www.smoochya.com**:

Win FREE books and makeup!
Read excerpts from other books!
Chat with the authors!
Horoscopes!
Quizzes!